tHe PRODIGAL

HAROLD RALEY

A Mouse Gate™ Adventure

Mouse Gate Press
1103 Middlecreek
Friendswood, TX 77546
281-992-3131 TEL
www.totalrecallpress.com

ISBN: 978-1-59095-340-2
UPC: 6-43977-43401-2

Library of Congress Control Number: 2016956842

Printed in the United States of America with simultaneous printings in Australia, Canada, and United Kingdom.

FIRST EDITION
1   2   3   4   5   6   7   8   9   10

To Vicky

The Author

Novelist, linguist, philosopher, and professor, Harold Raley holds degrees (BA, MA, Ph D) in English, Foreign Languages, Humanities, and Philosophy. He has taught in American and foreign universities. His books include fiction, history, language learning, and philosophy, and approximately 150 articles and columns on wide-ranging topics in professional journals and newspapers.

About the Book

In the tradition of Crusoe and Sabatini, *The Prodigal* is a story of the shipwreck and struggle for survival of a young ship's carpenter who escapes one captivity only to fall into more dangerous circumstances. The story unfolds from Boston to Mexico, Cuba, Africa, and back again. At critical points a mysterious stranger intervenes to lend a hand and guide him to his destiny.

CHAPTER I

"**N**athaniel, son, come back!" were the last words I ever heard my father say. They still echo in my memory as they echoed in the deep forests and ravines that surrounded the Tennessee town of Maryville, built on the site of our ancestral Cherokee village. I recall clearly how he stood by our tent, waving and repeating his plea until I was out of hearing. I turned only once to wave. Then I rapped my horse smartly with the bridle rein, urging him into a gallop up the mountain slope. The years have softened the discontent I felt at the moment and increased my nostalgia for the old matters of life forever lost in the past.

I could recite by heart the stories and names of my ancestors and the romance of my great great-grandparents Matthew and Agali Stokesbury. True to his promise to Chief Mardok, Great great-grandfather Matthew gathered books and materials and taught the tribe all he knew of the Christian faith, and with it the English tongue. Chief Mardok's two sons, born to his first wife, were always hostile to my great-great grandfather Matthew Stokesbury and abandoned our village, leaving Agali, though adopted, as his only surviving child. Eight years after my great-great parents were declared married according to tribal custom, Chief Mardok, who felt the burden of years upon him, adopted Matthew as his son and relied increasingly on his counsel.

Other tribesmen privately grumbled that a white man, a *unega*, was their chief in all but title. But none openly challenged Chief Mardok, who reminded them that all the chiefs who had borne the name for many generations were descendants of Mardok's son, the first *unega* chief. Thus it was that my great-great grandfather acted as a sub-chief during Mardok's final years. Before he died in the winter of 1694-95, "old and full of years," as Matthew recited from the Bible in his funeral eulogy, none protested when he declared that Matthew would be the next Chief. But he added the stipulation that from now on his title must also be his name. Thus after many generations, another Welshman, bearing the same name as the legendary first Mardok, was again chief of the Cherokee.

But if *unega* was a revered word in old Cherokee legend, it became a curse when between 1740 and 1750 lawless whites began crossing the mountains to raid, plunder, and murder. It was, I am sure, a personal burden for my great-grandfather, also named Nathaniel. He was the fairest of his siblings. His green eyes told not only of his paternal ancestry but perhaps reflected his grandmother's ancient European lineage as well, if the old legends could be believed. He protested when children began calling him *unega* ("whitey") but soon it became his tribal nickname, used alike by children and grownups, who found his English name hard to pronounce. His siblings Mary and Hamilton had no noticeable European features but greatly resembled instead the other Cherokee children. From the first he perceived that he was different and the perception convinced him that he would never be taken for a true Cherokee, chiefly perhaps because he did not think of himself as such. He devoured all the books he could come by, but chiefly those about travel and geography. I inherited his bookish trait and read everything I could lay hands on, included a few that remained from his time.

It was a mystery to me why my Grandfather never left the village to explore the world beyond the mountains. He died before I could ask him, and the family would give me no reasonable explanations. On the contrary, they responded angrily when I asked, which caused me to wonder if some unhappy family secret was behind the mystery. All they told me was that no one in their right mind would leave their homeland to venture out into the strange and hostile white world. Perhaps they were right, but the white world was absorbing or annihilating everything in its path. Soon there would be no place of safety left for those who wanted no part of it.

With one notable exception, most of my Cherokee people had little to do with the war of independence from England. The exception was my father Nathaniel who served as a scout for the rebel forces at the battle of King's Mountain. He was immediately hailed for his accurate information about the movement of the British forces. But as soon as the battle was over, he was dismissed with indifference and no small amount of scorn. He returned to Maryville, as our village was called by that time, an embittered man who never again wanted anything to do with whites, British or American.

After the war with England and the news that the American colonists had formed their own nation, the over-mountain raids increased and the whites began to settle and intermingle with our Cherokee people. This and the susceptibility of the Cherokees to the alcohol and diseases they brought soon reduced the pureblood Cherokees to a small minority. In my own case I am certain that my blood is more white than Cherokee, even though I could not document the legitimacy of my ancestral line. To tell the unhappy truth, many of the Cherokee women were violated and the men killed or destroyed by alcohol and disease. Although my eyes are blue and my beard almost as thick as those of white men, I have black Cherokee hair and skin a shade darker than most full-blood whites. Our tribal history was quickly disappearing; only a few elderly Cherokees still remembered the old language, and the young, myself included, chose to speak only English.

My father's desperate pleas for me to return grew fainter, but I did not pause. I had my life to live and he had his to finish. In spirit I had separated from the family long before the day I rode away on the dead Frenchman's pony, and unlike my Grandfather, I meant to make the break, not to think uselessly about it until my life was too far spent. My father spoke often of the workings of Providence. I paid little heed to his teachings and had my doubts about a God I could not see and who responded with silence to the prayers father taught us. As for the old Cherokee teachings that I remembered, I dismissed them as superstitions and myths.

Likewise, I disbelieved the stories about the legendary Madok. To me they were also the fanciful product of ignorance, like others that some of the old people still told us around hearth and campfire. Yet I did not object to the convenient thought that God ordained the death of the Frenchman Trémont in our village, who by his dying words made it clear that my father was to inherit the mare and her colt was to be mine.

This seems to be as good a time as any to say that should any of my family chance to read this account of my early life and wanderings, let them do so knowing that it is flawed in irremediable ways. The man I am now only partly continues to be the youth I was when most of these events occurred. It has always been a mystery to me—and another reason why I once had doubts about an all-wise God—why our most life-defining events seem to occur before we have the knowledge and skill to deal effectively with them. In the midst of youth and ignorance, we are obliged to deal the great perplexities of life. Perhaps our ancestral pagan gods still live and take delight in our confusion, tormenting us as children sometimes torture small animals. We claim the love of divine origin, but is that only because we fear to describe the real nature of things? At that time I had no answer to the question, nor have I yet, though my assertions have grown stronger, as they tend to do with old men.

And there is another problem. Many years have passed and while my faith has returned in great strength, I am not sure whether some of my toils and troubles were at all as I recall them. Instead they may consist of invented memories. Truth weakens like a drying stream as it stretches back into the past, and time often betrays memory with stronger fancies. With much time and much altering, perhaps like the Madok legends, stories sprout branches, roots, and fruits that were not part of the original, but now seem truer than what was real at the earlier and actual time. I claim no peculiarity for myself in these misgivings, for I see my friends and acquaintances with very different histories experiencing similar lapses, if indeed they can be called that.

But before I become hopelessly bogged down in soft-brained sentimentalities, let me return to the tale of my life. After a day's ride into the mountains, I entered unfamiliar terrain. As yet I had discerned no trace of white settlements, but guessed from what travelers had told me that they lay not far ahead of me. A thrill of fear and excitement gripped me. What would I find there? Danger? Fortune? None of the stories I knew prepared me, and as I learned later, none could have. For I was already past a point of no return and was soon to be subjected to dangers for which my most extravagant daydreams could not have forewarned or prepared me.

An hour before dusk, these and other idle thoughts came to an abrupt end. Suddenly three white men emerged from the trees. Before I could react, one jerked the reins from my hand and two others pulled me from the frightened horse and threw me to the ground. I looked up to see a musket aimed at my head.

"Could be Cherokee or a half-breed from the looks of his hair," said the tallest of the three. "Shoot him, Jake, or cut his throat and throw the body in the bushes, and bring the horse along. It's young and looks to be in good condition. We can sell or trade it or maybe keep it for our own use."

"But Jarvis, do you think that Harry Bradmore would give us money for the boy?" asked the shorter, thin-faced Jake.

"I doubt it. What would he be good for? When they're mountain bred and scrawny like this one they're not suitable for regular service or work."

"But he was riding a horse, and that's peculiar in itself," said the stocky, gray-bearded third man. "These mountain Indians don't have horses. Why don't you ask him how he came by the animal? There might be more where this one came from. You speak some Cherokee, don't you, Jarvis?"

"Some, but nowadays most of these mountain Cherokees, pure or mixed, speak some English."

The tall man started to ask me in butchered Cherokee, but I answered him in English. "A Frenchman, a fur trader on his way west, died in our village four years ago and left me the horse, then a colt. It is mine."

"Well, what dya know! He does speaks English," said the gray-beard, shaking his head.

"Yeah, and better than you, Frank," laughed Jake. "How come you speak such good English, boy? And what's your name?"

"I learned it from my folks. We're white. My name is Nathaniel Stokesbury."

"Big name for such a scrawny kid. But you know, Jarvis, he could be telling the truth. His skin is whiter than any Indian I ever saw, and now that I look at him up close, his eyes are blue and he's sprouting some beard. Who ever heard tell of a blue-eyed, bearded Indian?"

"Where was you headed when we caught you?" Jarvis asked, prodding me in the side with his boot.

I gave no answer.

"Boy, I asked you where you was heading," he said angrily, giving me a swift kick in the ribs.

"To Hampton," I gasped out the name of the only city that popped into my mind. By this time I fairly shook with fear that they would kill me, as the tall one called Jarvis had first threatened.

"And what's your business there?"

"To apprentice myself for a trade," I said, unable to think of a better answer. "I cannot live any longer in Cherokee country with the fighting and sickness. I am a white man, as you can see."

"I'd say you ain't no kind of a man yet," Jake laughed. "Hell, you ain't nobody, are you boy?"

I did not answer him.

"And mayhap never will be after we finish with you," Jake threatened.

"Tie him up," Jarvis ordered, "and tight so he don't run away while we're deciding what to do with him. Bradmore might take him off our hands at the Cumberland Camp. It's worth a try. And keep your eyes open, in case there are more of them out in the bush."

Jake tied my hands and feet with buckskin thongs. They talked out of my hearing for a while as my dread built up into near panic. Then gray-bearded Frank came back, untied my ankles, and ordered me to my feet. "You'll walk tied behind the horse, and you better hope he's broke good so that he don't spook. If he does and runs away, he'll drag you to your death over these rocks or leave you so battered that we'll have to do it for him."

"Why can't I ride my horse? You could tie him to your mount."

"You'll walk because that's what Jarvis says, and what he says goes. Don't cross him, boy. If he says jump, you better make like a jackrabbit."

"Where are you taking me?"

"You'll know when we get there. Now no more questions, because you'll get no more answers."

I walked for hours until the mounted whites camped for the night, chewing on dried venison and sharing water from a buckskin bag. Once the bearded man called Frank got up to offer me a cut of meat and a drink, but Jarvis stopped him.

"Frank, give him a drink but don't go wasting vittles on the boy. We're running short. He'll last till we get to the Cumberland Camp tomorrow or the next day, but if he drops aforehand, the forest varmints can feast on him."

"Why drag the kid along?" Jake said, "He's more trouble than he'll ever be profit to us. But I've been thinking about that horse and I sure could put it to good use."

"You leave horse and kid to me and stay a distance away if you know the good of it for you," Jarvis answered in a menacing tone. "I'm head man here and working out the profit is my business. And don't you forget it."

"I was just making talk, Jarvis," Jake whimpered.

We reached the Cumberland Camp around the middle of the third day. I was hungry, thirsty, and scratched but not really the worse for wear. In happier conditions I had walked much farther in the mountains. Frank tied my hands around a birch tree and served himself a sizeable piece of venison, grinning at me as he chewed but offering me nothing. Meanwhile Jarvis negotiated with two men in a large white tent. The tantalizing vapors tortured me with images of food and water.

Later Jarvis told me that I was to be hauled in an ox cart to a city named Williamsburg where I would appear before a magistrate to answer to a criminal charge.

"What crime? I have committed no crime."

"Oh, but you have, boy. What about the horse you stole from me? There it is, plain as day."

"But, sir, the horse is mine!"

"I have two witnesses that will swear it's mine. Can you prove them wrong? You got documents proving ownership of the animal?"

It happened as Jarvis said it would. After two and half days of bouncing overland in an ox cart and four more locked in a Williamsburg jail, a black-robed Williamsburg magistrate declared me guilty—of stealing my own horse—and sentenced me to a public whipping and six months of incarceration.

"You got off light, boy," a constable whispered in my ear. "Maybe because you're young and mostly white, so they tell me. You could have received a hanging sentence."

At that moment a tall, corpulent man rose in the attending public and asked to address the magistrate.

"Sir, I shall hear you only if it pertains to the matter with which we are presently occupied."

"It does indeed pertain to the matter at hand, your honor. With respect, I am Harry Bradmore, son of John Bradmore, of the Hampton Bradmores. I come in representation of my father who regrets that ill health prevents him from appearing in person before you."

"The esteemed Mr. John Bradmore is favorably known to this court, and as his son and representative, you are received cordially in his name. Please explain, sir, the business that brings you before us."

"Your honor, if it please the court, on behalf of my father I am instructed to pay all fines and public expenses incurred in the arrest, incarceration, trial, and conviction of the felon Nathaniel Stokesbury yonder seated and request in consequence that he be turned over to my father's estate in indentured servitude for a period of time that this court in its wisdom will see fit to set. My father has authorized me to declare on his honor as a gentleman that the fellow shall be treated humanely and shall do honest labor to compensate for the crime committed, all the while obeying the principles and rules of Christian behavior."

"The court so rules, taking into account the disposition of Mr. John Bradmore and stipulating the following conditions. Let the court records show that the prisoner is hereby sentenced for a period not less or more than five years to the service and supervision of Mr. John Bradmore or his agents subsequent to payment of fines and costs, as Mr. Harry Bradmore has stated. The prior sentence is accordingly set aside, subject to re-imposition of the same or to graver punishment should this court become cognizant of further unlawful acts by this person."

The following months now appear to contract to a much shorter time. Yet for nearly a full year I labored with a baker's dozen of indentured Irish and Scottish servants on the Hampton plantations belonging first to the elder Bradmore and, upon his death several months later, passing by inheritance to his son Harry Bradmore.

An incident during my second year of servitude that set the course of my life on a new and unexpected pathway. As son and heir to the Bradmore estate and fortune, Harry Bradmore set about ambitiously to reorganize his plantations and servants. Having proved myself to be an adept worker, I was released from my dull task as herdsman in the back pastures and plantations near Hampton to join an experienced cadre on a vast plantation near Williamsburg where Bradmore himself had resettled his family in an opulent residence. There he named me apprentice to his blacksmith Hiram Hardin, a squint-eyed, emaciated man who drank rum constantly and paid little attention to me. The work was much more to my liking than the lonely work in the pastures, and only a few months passed before I surpassed my indolent master in working with iron, brass, and other metals, and showed considerable skill in woodwork. Far from resenting my emerging skills, the indifferent and steadily weakening Hardin heaped more work on me and devoted his time to his rum bottle, his only friend and consolation.

It so happened that Mistress Brenda Bradmore, wife of Harry Bradmore, prevailed on her husband to install at the entry lane to their estate an elaborate metal gate with family insignia. For she claimed that the Bradmores were descended from English aristocracy. Obligingly he ordered Hardin to proceed with the design and installation. But now sunk in nearly permanent rummy drunkenness, Hardin's design was a flawed travesty of competent workmanship. Bradmore was irate when he saw the work and ordered his overseer to summarily dismiss him—with a flogging if he resisted. The drunken Hardin went quietly, but now Bradmore was in a quandary, lacking a craftsman and further than ever from having a presentable gate. Daily he suffered vain Mistress Bradmore's unrelenting hysterical outcries that their social standing must become subject to ridicule when the gentry and authorities from Williamsburg saw the rubbish that Hardin called a gate.

In desperation Bradmore turned to me as the only possibility in the short time left. "Think you, Stokesbury, that you could design and install such a gate? I am mindful that you have shown skill in working with metal and wood. But mind you, we have only a fortnight," he reminded me. Then, turning away, he added almost in a whisper under his breath, "Not that I shall live so long unless something is done to soothe her harpy temper."

I assured him that I could, and in a bare ten days I produced and installed a princely gate complete with the family coat of arms that greatly pleased both skeptical Bradmores. In my impatient, youthful hope, I dared think that in consequence of this triumphant work and the favorable display of my talents, Bradmore might release me from further servitude and even offer me Hardin's position, which carried, as I believed, a modest stipend. But his natural avarice and meanness of spirit proved stronger than any impulse of gratitude. I was told by one of the older servants that it was a Bradmore trait, evident in earlier generations of the family. He offered not a word of thanks or hint of recompense. I saw my fate handwritten on the wall. Years of unappreciated, unpaid labor lay ahead of me. And perhaps more, for my disillusioning experience with Williamsburg justice fed my suspicions that new accusations could be leveled against me at any time with the same ease as in the first false charge, so that my servitude could extend for as long I proved profitable to Bradmore and the dishonest magistrates. I was learning the hard way to foresee in the character of men a prophetic chart of their future acts. From the moment that realization settled into my thinking I began making plans to slip away from Bradmore's greedy grasp. For the briefest moment I entertained the thought of running back to my family in the mountains. But the thought quickly faded. The world now belonged to the whites whose dominion was broad and tyrannical. But surely, I reasoned, somewhere in it a better destiny awaited me.

My best chance for escape was even now upon me and I was obliged to move hastily. The inaugural ball drew all attention and ordinary surveillance ceased in favor of the great event. I gathered my meager belongings and a few coins that in his drunken haze Hardin had neglected to pocket. Then, having packed away as much food as I could lay hands on, I slipped out into the night, leaving by the new gate after the last arriving carriages had rumbled past. For a moment I was tempted to unhinge the gate and drag it to the middle of the lane as a vengeful gesture to embarrass Bradmore and his frivolous lady. But then I thought better of it; anger was a poor reason to damage my own good work. Perhaps my father's teaching legacy had a greater weight than I knew, for even at that young impulsive age I was already persuaded that vengeance is but a second helping from the menu of wrongdoing.

I had daydreamed much but thought little in concrete of a better destination, but I recalled that one of the indentured Irish servants, by name Owen O' Farrell, had told me of the docks and great ships he had seen upon his arrival in Salem, Massachusetts. His descriptions stirred my imagination. My mind could not yet feature the unbounded sea, yet from there, I reasoned, I could travel to the farthest reaches of the world. I had never sailed, but for everything there is a first time. I would head for Salem, and from there circumstances yet unborn would determine my next step.

Daylight brought with it the fear of recapture. I was now a fugitive, and recalling the magistrate's warning of harsher punishment should I fail to abide by the terms of my sentence, I decided to shorten my names from Nathaniel to Nathan, and Stokesbury to the simpler Stokes. It was a feeble disguise for anyone bent on discovering my true identity, but all I could think of under the circumstances.

CHAPTER 2

I shall omit several phases of my journey to Massachusetts, but what happened to me in Boston bears telling. Two weeks later, hungry and cold, I fairly staggered into that city. I had slept in forests and abandoned buildings and eaten roots and berries, and cadged carriage rides when I could. For once I was grateful for the forest lore my Cherokee relatives had taught me. Would that I had listened more closely to my elders!

It was too late in the season to reach Salem. Autumn was far advanced, winter soon to descend, and I knew not when, if ever, the next morsel of food would touch my lips. I could go no further. To my inquiries framed in complete ignorance of Boston and its people and in a strange accent, I received curt dismissals from passersby and warnings by the alerted constables to cease molesting decent folk.

My appearance was also a curse on my cause. My clothing was now dirty and beginning to fray and my hair too long and black to win me a sympathetic hearing from the prosperous fair-skinned and tawny-haired Bostonians. During a respite from their unfriendly scrutiny, I wandered about city's forty-acre Common, desperately hungry and anxiously considering my circumstances. Late in the day, a Monday if I recall rightly, I passed a corpulent man with a shock of red hair sitting on a bench and amusing himself by tossing nuts and grains to a veritable tribe of raucous, fluttering birds and chittering, scampering squirrels. His clothing was of an elegant but antique cut. On his right ring finger a large gold ring with a magnificent blue turquoise caught my attention, for the Cherokee and other native people believe it to be a lucky stone. I thought to myself how grateful I should be to join the beasts and consume some of the precious grains and nuts myself. The first time I passed by, the man gave me not the slightest glance. Then on my reverse circuit, he called after me in a deep baritone voice.

"I say there, Nathan, attend me!"

"Sir?" I responded, astonished that he knew me by name but fearful, judging by his sharp tone, that I had in some manner either offended him or been discovered as the fugitive I had become. Not far behind me strolled a pair of constables eyeing my movements.

"Step this way, I would have a word with you."

"Yes sir, but how is it that you know my name? I have never seen you before. But how may I be of service to you?" I asked as I watched the constables out of the corner of my eye.

"How I know your abbreviated name is of no consequence. You cannot serve me in any way you could imagine, but I may be of some aid to you. What are your intentions in Boston?"

I hesitated but saw no reason to ignore his request. He seemed to know everything about me already, and knew the answers before he asked the questions. "I hoped to apprentice myself as a metal worker and carpenter in Salem, but the weather and circumstances obliged me to stop here in Boston."

"From the looks of you, I venture to say hunger was the main one," he laughed. "So thin have you become that you fain must stand twice to cast a single shadow."

His words annoyed me and too hungry to entertain frivolous commentaries about my condition, I said nothing in response. For a long moment neither did he as he eyed me intensely. Then he extracted from a vest pocket three small coins—gold by their look—and proffered them. "Take these coins; the first will be more than enough to have your hair and whiskers trimmed in yon barbershop by the upper Common, and the return change will suffice for several day's lodging and board in the neighboring inn. On the morrow when merchants open their doors for business procure for yourself decent clothing. The remaining coins shall do you until you earn your first wage."

"Wage? Sir, what wage?" I said irritably. "I have no employment, nor prospects of any."

"Be patient, Nathan. Betake yourself thereafter to the wharf address I shall give thee and speak to owner Gaylord Stafford. He rises early and attends to many matters, so do not delay, lest the opportunity pass you by. You must speak to owner Gaylord himself. Be not dismayed by his assistant who delights in bullying all such as you. Understand you my instructions?"

"Yes sir. But why, I ask, are you doing this? You are not known to me, even though in some manner that is a mystery to me you know my name."

He smiled broadly and tossed another handful of feed to the fluttering birds and scurrying squirrels at his feet. "Indeed, your knowledge is limited, yet it is important that you follow my instructions. Now see to your tasks, lad, as I have described them to you, as I must see to mine."

So saying, he handed me the bag of grain and nuts and walked away quickly across the common as the constables reached me. I turned to go also, but one of the men called to me.

"A word with you, fellow. What have you in the bag?"

"Why the grain and nuts the gentleman seated here was

tossing to the birds and squirrels."

"Gentleman? Look about you, fellow" said the older constable. "There is no one on the Common save the three of us at this late hour. Nor has there been in the past hour. We have been watching as you gestured as though speaking to someone. Are you drunk with grog? We must know your business. You appear to be an idler without worthwhile purpose here. Let me see what the bag contains."

"Certainly. The gentleman was, as I said, tossing grain and nuts to the birds and squirrels. And as for me, I am Nathan Stokes, and I am in Boston for the purpose of apprenticing myself as an ironworker or carpenter."

He opened the bag, and seeing that the contents were as I described, frowned and returned it. "Now, do you have lodging or money to arrange it or shall you be our guest in our jail?"

"Indeed I have money, good sirs, and will straightway attend to the matter if you will give me leave to do so," I responded, showing the officers one of my three gold coins.

They looked at each other, apparently in disbelief that I had money, but finding no reason to query me further, instructed me not to appear again on Boston streets in such shameful array. I was more eager to comply than they could have guessed.

I hoped to thank the benevolent stranger, but he was nowhere to be seen. I dared not linger on the Common lest the annoyed constables lose patience and carry out their threat to jail me. In any case, surely I would see the gentleman again under better circumstances and thank him for his charity. Meanwhile, making my way to the barbershop, I munched on the nuts and grains as ravenously as the hungriest members of the feathered and furry tribes had done not long before me.

After my hair and whiskers were properly trimmed—not without unwelcome commentary by the barber—I ventured with considerable trepidation into the inn. I was unacquainted with such places and my appearance, though improved by the barber, inspired little confidence. The innkeeper looked me up and down with suspicious reluctance, but persuaded by a shiny gold coin, gave me room and board in his establishment, returning several lesser silver coins in change. After devouring a hot chowder and scrubbing my body, I slept the sleep of death.

The next day was well advanced when I awoke with a start, and remembering how the redheaded man had described the busy Mr. Stafford, I hastened to a nearby clothing store and quickly purchased new garments for myself. By midmorning I presented myself to his establishment only to be confronted by his officious assistant who ordered me to leave. But I stubbornly held my ground, having been forewarned by my benefactor and determined to speak only to Mr. Stafford.

Angered by my obstinate refusal to depart, the assistant raised his voice and threatened to expel me by main strength, for he was bigger and better fed than I. At that moment the inner door slammed against the wall and a large, red-haired man entered.

"What is all this commotion?" he said to the assistant in a rumbling, baritone voice. "I could hear your shouting from the far end of the shop."

"Sir, this fellow will not quit the premises, even though I ordered him to do so."

"And why, lad, do you make an obstinate ass of yourself?" he asked, turning to me.

"I am no ass, sir. I was told to come here and to speak only to you."

"Who told you such? I do not know you. What is your name?"

"He would not state his business, Mr. Stafford," the assistant said angrily, "and to be sure he has none worthy of your attention."

"Sir, I am Nathan Stokes, at your service. The name of the gentleman who so instructed me is surely known to you, though he did not give his name to me. I can offer you only a description of his person. He is a hefty, well-dressed man with very red hair like yours who spoke of you in familiar terms. By the resemblance, I now see that possibly he is your kinsman. He summoned me to him on the Common as he was feeding grain and nuts to the animals."

"What other particulars about this man can you give me? What you have told me could variously describe a hundred Bostonians."

"I recollect only that on the fourth finger of his right hand he wore a gold ring with a large turquoise mounting. And his voice was deep like yours, sir."

Mr. Stafford paled at my description and spoke words under his breath that I could not catch.

"Sir?" asked the assistant, whose name I learned later was Steadman Fuller.

"Never you mind, Fuller. Leave me alone with this young man. I will hear him out."

Fuller gave me a hateful look and took his time leaving as ordered. Once we were alone, Mr. Stafford queried me at length about the redheaded man. But I could add little to what I had told him earlier.

"That will do, Stokes," he said abruptly, holding up his hand to stop me. "Why did you come to see me?"

"Sir, I would like to apprentice myself to you as a metalworker and learn what I can of carpentry."

"I myself am proficient in neither of those crafts. But to conclude the matter, for reasons I will not explain, I am willing to take you on as apprentice in my shop under the conditions that commonly pertain in these arrangements. These include food and an occasional wage. For lodging you may accommodate yourself in the loft over the shop. Heat from the forges will keep you warm enough in winter, but you must take your meals elsewhere, for the space has neither heating nor cooking stove. Showing up when you did is strangely convenient. We are in need of a helper, and it is possible I know the man who sent you to me. His recommendation, for such I take it, must serve. You shall begin at once under the guidance and instruction of Master Thomas Olgivie. But bear in mind, Stokes, if you prove to be indolent or talentless I shall be obliged to dismiss you forthwith. And now that we have finished our talk, I have other tasks. Come, I shall take you to Master Olgivie."

"Sir, I cannot thank you enough and promise that I shall obey faithfully all that you and Master Olgivie instruct me to do. And I would like to thank the gentleman who sent me to you. Can you tell me his name and where to find him?"

"I could tell you only who I believe he is, but for reasons you would not understand, I shall not do so. In any case, I could not tell you how to find him. But if he is of a mind to do so, he will find you."

"I don't understand, sir."

"Be grateful for his help, but to the little I have told you, Stokes, I will add no more. Now come with me and make the acquaintance of Master Olgivie."

Master Olgivie, a tall muscular Scot of middling years with a close-clipped red beard, stern look, and intense blue eyes proved to be a man of balanced disposition, yet exacting to a fault in all things pertaining to his craft. It troubled me that prudence would not permit me to provide him details of my experience on the Bradmore estate in Virginia, but I assured him in Mr. Stafford's hearing that even though I could not claim a high level of mastery in metallurgy and carpentry, I promised to be ready and willing to learn.

"He seems fit," he said to Stafford, and turning to me, added, "now, lad, let us see if your work proves to be as good as your words."

Although it will come as no surprise to readers acquainted with my full account, Master Olgivie and Mr. Stafford, knowing nothing of my servitude in Virginia, marveled in the following days at the speed with which I demonstrated skill in both metals and wood. Not many days passed before Master. Oligivie, now my advocate, assigned me the task of forging precisely dimensioned iron bolts and shaping matching planking for the skeletal hull of a two-masted schooner rounding into shape in a dry dock adjacent to the workshop.

Despite further queries and searches in Boston, I learned nothing more about my mysterious redheaded benefactor. But years later in a land half a world away I was destined to meet him again, and to be as baffled by our second encounter as I was mystified by the first.

Master Thomas Olgivie and his wife Sarah, were the parents

of seven children, in ages when I first met them from eight to twenty. Frederick, 20, the eldest, soon became my good friend and working companion in the shop. Master Oligivie, the son of Matthew Oligivie and Nattie Mckenzie Oligivie, made no distinction between us insofar as the quality of our labor was concerned; on the contrary, only the very best we were capable of was acceptable. And our best was never singularly praiseworthy; invariably he pointed to some minute flaw that only his eagle eye could see. Yet because his hard exterior could not hide a much nobler heart, I came to respect him all the more.

Mrs. Oligivie was a highland Scottish lady. At first I missed the meaning of some of her oddly intoned words. But her maternal warmth and concern for my welfare were unmistakable. She all but adopted me as another chick in her brood and thought it a tragedy of nature that I was separated from my own family. (I said little of the circumstances.) Only a heartless person could have failed to respond to her warmth. And even if her motherly affection had failed to win through, her food and table would have tamed the stoniest heart.

I believe Master Olgivie, as she always called her husband in public, felt obliged to maintain a certain patriarchical severity lest the whole family risk dissolution into a saccharine maternal mush. But it was not lost on any of us that he adored his wife.

Jane, newly turned eighteen when I met her, captivated me from the start. Tall, redheaded, with sky-blue eyes, delicate features and pearl-white complexion, she was the most beautiful girl I had ever seen. She did all things with a happy exuberance that never failed to lift me out of my customary silence and cause my face to crease in unused smiles, though often I was tongue-tied in her presence. I could not at that inexperienced age give my feelings their rightful name, but from the higher elevation of advancing years, I now recognize it as love of her at first sight, as the Romantic poets call it.

In even numbers but alternating sexes came Kevin, 16, Alice, 14, Joseph, 12, Madilyn, 10, and Ramsey, 8. Though I spoke little of my life in the southern mountains, the little I said stirred their curiosity. They plied me with questions and as my affection for the family grew, and in a special, secret way for Jane, so did my trust. I revealed more of my history to them.

One night as Mrs. Olgivie was serving us a rich pot roast, Frederick laid his hand on my arm and asked, "Nathan, from what you say, your family must have Indian ancestry."

Mrs. Olgivie stopped and waited for my response. I would have preferred to remain silent but knew now I could not. With a measure of annoyance and an admixture of fear, and excepting my full name, I opted for honesty.

"Not Indian, which includes a variety of peoples, good and bad. My family is of white and Cherokee descent, and the Cherokee consider themselves to be what you might call the most advanced of the original Americans. My Great grandmother was Cherokee, my great grandfather Welsh, born in the old country," I said, looking at Jane as I spoke. My grandfather, after whom I am named, married a Whitcomb of English ancestry. "But whatever that makes me, I am myself in all plainness and without pretense, Nathan Stokes."

Mrs. Olgivie put down her serving ladle and walked around the table to give me a hug with kind words I always treasured. "You are our friend, Nathan, and I am pleased that you are supping with us. The Lord's blessing be on you now and always, for your being here is his holy doing. We are all his sons and daughters, and we must take pride in our ancestry and honor our forefathers. For God created all the races of man for his glory and purpose."

"Mother Olgivie, as always you speak the truth," said Master Olgivie. Then he went to say, "Nathan, your heritage be one thing, your craft another, though there be connections not visible. See that you continue to work earnestly. Mr. Stafford has placed a trust in you and put you under my guidance for instruction. If in any way you see your heritage as a hindrance, conform to what Mother Olgivie said. And look all the more to your craft so as to honor and fulfill the trust placed in you and thereby to praise your Creator and raise yourself in the eyes and esteem of men."

"That, sir, I shall try to do in every way," I answered, ill at ease.

"Now, having said what must needs be said," Master Olgivie declared in a lighter tone, rare for him, "Mother, please serve your excellent pot roast! And note ye well, Nathan and Frederick, and all present besides, if ye should learn to do your tasks as well as Mother Olgivie knows her cooking, ye shall indeed be deemed masters of your craft!"

We all broke into spontaneous applause and cries of "Hear! Hear!" Mother Olgivie's happy face blushed pink with pleasure as she rounded the table to hug and kiss each and all in turn.

Dark, wintery Boston at length began its spring surrender to light and warmth, in joyful cadence with my own radiant and rising happiness. I was in deeply in love with Jane and everything bright and beautiful reminded me of her. The center of my life moved away from my old morbid thoughts about myself and settled in her. Boston was beautiful because she was there to make it so. The plainest streets and shops took on an afterglow because she had walked along them. I had never dreamed before that life could be so good, and caught up in her magic, everything I once saw as dreary and dead now sparkled with magical meaning. For the first time I sensed that I was coming into my own. By some wonderful, paradoxical magic, by centering my life in her I was becoming myself. And I forgot my old quarrels with God.

But there were fearful, tormenting questions: Did Jane love me? Could she love me? What would she say if I became bold enough to confess my love to her, as I knew I must sooner or later? She was my friend, of that I could have no doubt. All the Olgivies, modeling themselves on Mother Olgivie, lavished friendship in all the noble, magnificent range of sentiment the word could contain. But was that friendship destined to be a boundary, perhaps even the enemy of my love for Jane? I dreaded a fallback from the full grace of her love, a retreat to lesser glories and a compromise with what I foresaw as perfect happiness.

The schooner was in the main completed, wanting only the completion of the upper decking being shipped down from Portland in the Maine territory and a dozen cannons in transport from England. In the meantime, our shop carpenters and mechanics, reputed to be the best in New England, constructed a handsome pinnacle to serve as the schooner's boat.

Frederick and I could not keep our eyes and hands off the smaller princely vessel, and as soon as it was seaworthy he began to implore his father to let us take it out for a shakedown cruise in Boston Bay. As first Master Olgivie simply ignored his son's pleas, but at length, wearied of Frederick's requests, he called us to him and explained that since the pinnacle was not his, he could not authorize its use.

"You must approach Mr. Stafford on the matter, though were it up to me, I should say no to entrusting such an expert craft to inexperienced hands. And prepare ye for a like response from Mr. Stafford. If he denies permission, as most assuredly he will, the matter shall be settled without further ado."

But Mr. Stafford had a better idea.

"I believe the young men have hit upon the right idea," he said to Master Olgivie, "but perhaps without providing sufficient crew and passengers for the excursion. Let us declare this very Saturday a day of recreational pleasure to celebrate the pinnacle and the schooner. And even though for the latter, which stills lacks its finishing touches, the festivities are a trifle early, the weather bids fair to be ideal and spirits are high because of labor all but finished and, if I do say so, expertly done. We shall staff the pinnacle with family, employees, a pair of expert sailors, and with abundant drink and food take a gay turn about the Bay. What say you?"

We were delighted. Even stern Master Olgivie smiled at the pleasant prospect. As for me, I was eager to be close to Jane. Perhaps, I smiled to myself, I could arrange matters unnoticed to sit next to her. I could imagine nothing more ideal.

The day turned out to be more pleasurable than we could imagine. The pinnacle responded deftly as we sailed smartly past the inner islands, waving or shouting to fishermen on their way to the Outer Banks. In the outer bay the swells and waves were larger, and as they struck, as though to test her, the pinnacle lifted and plunged through the watery valleys and peaks, involuntarily throwing us together. Mother Olgivie raised her frightened voice in prayer. Of her own accord, Jane had seated herself next to me, and though we said little each to the other, the feeling of her body pressing against me at those exciting moments was a heady sensation I shall never forget. As for Frederick, he was so thrilled with his first experience at steering and learning the intricacies of sailing that he spent nearly every minute learning what he could from the sailors.

The pinnacle stood a short distance off Point Allerton as the sailors, with Frederick's help, secured the vessel with two ship cables fore and aft tied to an old dock. This was to be the midpoint of our circular trajectory. Then we waded ashore with Mother Olgivie, all loaded with baskets of food and drink she had prepared for the crew and passengers. The salt air had so sharpened our appetite that we ate and drank until it seemed we would never again relish the smell and savor of food. Afterward, Jane and I, joined by her excited younger siblings, went along the shore to explore and look for seashells. At one point she took me by the hand as her brothers and sisters called me to explore a small cave they had discovered several hundred yards down the narrow peninsula.

"Forget that muddy cave, Nathan," she said with an impish smile. "Today you belong to me."

I thought my heart would pound through my breast at her words, and it is doubtful whether at that moment any human force could have pried me from her side.

It would take a volume to recount all the events and sensational emotions of that day and of many others in the long, lovely Boston spring and summer. To a casual observer they would have no doubt seemed trite, the trivial recollections of ordinary lives. But experienced from within, they were magical.

But pleasure pursued past the bounds of legitimacy has a way of turning nightmarish. With these ominous words as prologue, let me summarize what happened next.

In late July, Mr. Stafford purchased another shipbuilding enterprise in the town of Essex, and in the company of the expert Master Olgivie journeyed there to inspect and regulate it to his satisfaction. Master Olgivie gave us detailed instructions about our tasks and responsibilities. But as it was likely that they would need to spend several weeks in Essex, we readily agreed to our tasks while secretly reserving ample time for more pleasurable activities. Steadman Fuller was given the general charge of overseeing the shop during their absence. But since I loathed the man for the way he had treated me, and Frederick believed he surpassed him in standing because of his father's position, we promised to comply but perhaps not to obey fully.

Would that we had made a stronger resolve to see to our responsibilities! But as soon as Mr. Stafford and Master Olgivie were out of sight, their instructions were all but out of mind, replaced by Frederick's consuming passion to take the pinnacle out for another go in Boston Bay. I protested feebly against the idea, but secretly I was nearly as eager as Frederick, though concerned that a day at sea would mean a day away from Jane.

Two days later, a Wednesday, after stowing food and drink aboard the pinnacle, we slipped out of the harbor at first light. The "Rover," as Frederick had privately christened her, unburdened by the weight of so many people this time out, fairly skipped to a good breeze over the rippling bay. Distant clouds sat low on the eastern horizon but the sun was warm, our masters far removed, and the pinnacle's double sails as responsive and nimble as a thorough-bred horse.

Then standing off Point Allerton we debated turning back or racing ahead toward Cape Cod.

"But Frederick," I protested, "Cape Cod is too far to reach and return in a day, if I read the charts aright. Let's not press our luck. I don't have a good feeling about it."

"Feelings, smeelings! Don't be a chicken, Nathan! We'll race down and back to Boston and no one will be the wiser that we did. It will be a grand adventure!"

Seeing that Frederick had his mind firmly made up and aware of his Scottish stubbornness, I said no more. For several hours it appeared that he was right, but as we swung round and tacked north, the low lying clouds to eastward suddenly seem to awaken and move toward us like living things. The wind picked up and the pinnacle shook with the gusts. Hourly they grew in intensity and by midafternoon, as I judged the time, they reached gale force. Neither of us knew how to deal with the storm, and our ignorance was to be our undoing.

The clouds turned the day into darkness and soon rain came with such blinding volume and force that we lost all sense of direction. The pinnacle began to take in water faster than we could bail it as the gentle waves of the morning became the roaring monsters of the angry afternoon.

The occurred the worst. The wind and waves worked themselves into a simultaneous coordinated fury, capsizing the pinnacle and hurling us into the water. I saw Frederick go under an instant before the waves rose and smashed me into the deep. Fighting my way back to the surface and spitting mouthfuls of salty water, I called for him. But I heard no human voice above the screaming din of the storm. Unlike Frederick, an expert swimmer, I could barely swim at all, having learned to stay afloat in the freshwater creeks of my native Tennessee. But with great effort I made my way around the overturned craft. There was no sign of Frederick and no response to my cries. A cable from the toppled mast sail lashed about in the water. Grabbing it, I then ventured out as far as its length permitted, but still I heard nothing and saw only one of our two wicker food baskets being quickly carried away in the roiling current. The other was nowhere to be seen. Tiring and in danger of sinking into the deep myself, reluctantly I swam back to the capsized pinnacle, its keel barely visible a few inches below water level. Frederick, I concluded to my horror, had surely drowned.

Unbeknownst to me, overcome by panic, despair, and the howling gale, all the while the wind and surf were carrying the wreck and me shoreward. Thus it was that perhaps no more an hour passed before, to my surprise, my feet touched bottom and I waded out and collapsed on shore.

As morning dawned and the storm passed, I discovered myself to be on a fair sandy beach from where not far inland I espied wagons and carriages passing along a main high road. I inquired of a black-clad driver who stopped his team to stare me up and down, still wet and dripping salt water. But before giving me an answer, he desired to know how I came to be there. I pointed to the capsized pinnacle and spoke of the story, but gave only enough details to satisfy his curiosity and without mentioning the tragedy with Frederick, lest he should inform authorities. He said I was not far from the old town of Plymouth, famous, he proudly added, as the site where the English had first landed in New England.

He took me to Plymouth, pointed me to the northward running road to Boston, and drove away. I stood there undecided and mulling my options for a time. I was torn by powerful but opposing impulses. On the one hand, I desired above all else to see Jane again. But on the other, I dreaded having to tell Mother Olgivie and the family about Frederick's drowning and my irresponsible part in causing it. If I had stood firm, he could not have sailed alone in the pinnacle. There was no way I could stay in Boston. Even if the family and Mr. Stafford could forgive me for my part in the tragedy, I would be a daily reminder of their loss. I had lost my best friend, and now I must lose the girl I loved with all my heart. My world had capsized, as surely as the pinnacle, and everything was upside down. I thought of simply vanishing without telling the Olgivies, but conscience would not let me cowardly slink away. Besides, even though I bore a responsibility, I was not guilty of Frederick's death. As hard as it was, I must face the family and admit my complicity. I was aware that very likely their grief would be so much greater than mine than they could have no spare compassion for me, even if I had deserved it. I would be the living reminder of a brainless act that took Frederick's life. I could not stay in Boston, but for that same reason I must not leave without facing them like the man they once thought me to be.

And so I did the very next day. Mother Olgivie, frantic with worry before, now paled and with Jane's help stumbled to her bed at the news. I could hear her sobbing. At first the younger children did not understand what was wrong. Later they cried in a mixed confusion of disbelief and mourning for their beloved elder brother. Half an hour later Jane came out and gave me a long searching look but said nothing at first. Finally she asked me for details of the tragedy.

"We shall have to give an account to father and Mr. Stafford when they return," she said quietly.

"I can lead them to the beach where the pinnacle beached itself."

"That won't necessary, Nathan. By the time they return likely either the sea will have carried it away or salvagers taken it. Simply tell me the location and I shall relay the information."

"I want to do all I can to help."

"There is no real help any of us can offer now. Frederick is gone, and life must go on for those who remain."

"Jane, I want you to know that I did all in my power to find him."

"Nathan, no one doubts your good intentions and earnest efforts, but the fact remains that my brother is dead. Please pardon me for saying it, for it sounds cruel, but we will be reminded of his loss each time we see you."

"I have thought hard on that point, Jane, and I believe the best thing for all concerned is to remove myself so as not to be a painful reminder."

She nodded and after a silence spoke words that pierced my heart. "We had many things to tell each other, Nathan, and the time had not yet come for us to say them. Now they must never be said but silenced as things that can never be."

"Please do not hate me."

"I shall never hate you, Nathan, but instead always think of you as our friend. There is no room for hatred in this family. We shall, each and all, pray that your life be long and happy. I speak for Mother, Father, and all the family. But that is all I can say and all that should be said. Now, as you said, it is best that you leave Boston—and us."

The air was heavy with dampness as I stepped out into the dark street. A carriage rumbled past, iron rims and horseshoes harshly striking the cobblestones. There was no softness left in the world, and my destiny was as unknown to me as the destination of the carriage disappearing into the gloom.

Rather than spend the night in my quarters over the shop, I gathered my few possessions and lodged myself in the same inn on the Common where I had stayed upon my arrival in Boston. If it had a name, I cannot remember it.

I awoke to a monumental melancholy, but at least my unhappy obligations in Boston were settled and the thought of them almost tranquil, as though belonging to a time already long past. It steadied me that I had resolved my doubts about my next step. I would try my fortune in Salem, which had been my original destination.

CHAPTER 3

In the course of my life I have come to the conclusion that by comparing them each city will reveal a peculiar nature that colors and outlives the personal character of its mortal inhabitants. So it was with Salem. Compared to proud, firmly planted Boston, which gave the appearance and had the feel of a much older city than its calendar date, Salem, though of nearly equal history by year count, rested uneasily on its foundations, and one could not escape the impression that about it hovered an atmosphere of furtiveness and a stronger presence that I could only describe as shamefulness. I knew something of its nefarious history of witch hunts and superstitions, and no doubt that intelligence of the place colored my impressions. I sensed a collective guilt. On the other hand, I do not discount the possibility that I simply misread circumstances and again fell victim to my usual tendency to exaggerate. My knowledge, sparse as it is, is not rooted in formal instruction and thus lacks the necessary correction that wise schoolmasters can impart, but is instead the fruit of a disorderly and desultory assortment of readings and unguided philosophies. It is as though a library had crumbled at my feet, strewing books in wide disarray without sensible transitions or connections. Simply put, my thinking links concepts that have no business being lumped together.

The wharves buzzed with the busy hum of men as great schooners, whalers, and clippers disgorged cargoes and took on provisions for voyages to the ends of the earth. The bustle worked to my advantage. When shipmaster Eric Johnson, Captain of the clipper *Chesapeake,* learned that I had apprenticed under Master Ogilvie of Boston in the double crafts of iron work and carpentry, he quickly added me to his shorthanded crew without asking many questions about my skills and experience. It struck me as odd but suited my purposes. Officially the *Chesapeake* was bound for Jamaica, but secretly also had a second destination, as I learned later.

The readers of this account will understand my melancholy sentiments, especially as long as we were in Massachusetts waters to remind me of the pinnacle disaster. But the *Chesapeake* with its two rakish masts and rigging was famed for its speed and with steady winds and good seas in three days we were far down the coast. But to my wounded sentiments another problem was added: *mal de mer*, or to call it by its humbler English name, seasickness. Despite my lies about experience at sea, the veteran sailors quickly discerned by my gait that I lacked sea legs. Aboard the pinnacle we were never, or perhaps only briefly, out of sight of land. But on the open seas all such fixed terrestrial points were lacking and I was at the mercy of that other earth, the greater, unfixed world of the seas. For the better part of two days I was forced to endure not only vomiting miseries that seemed only a step from death itself but also the jokes and humiliations generously heaped on me by the hardened, callous sailors.

Chief among my tormentors was our Portuguese first mate Manuel Furtado, who from the first took a perverse pleasure in humiliating me in front of the others. But I soon discovered that I was not the only target of his vicious temperament. Many of the sailors despised him for his brutal ways and told unflattering stories about him as we gathered for water around the scuttlebutt. But six or seven of the fifteen-man crew were loyal to him for reasons I could not understand, for only four of them were Portuguese or Brazilian. It made even less sense to me that Captain Johnson would take on such a man as his first mate. To my sorrow I was to discover later the reasons and consequences of the decision.

Several times I inquired about our cargo, for during my inspection tours as carpenter's helper I was shown only our ship's stores in the hold. Durward Mason, the stooped and gray-grizzled ship's carpenter, took me aside and cautioned me to curb my curiosity.

"Lad, take some friendly advice. Word got up to the Captain about your questions. He's an able captain but hard, and he does not like a questioning crew. And Mate Furtado even less. God help you if that one finds you poking around below decks without good reason, there's no telling what he might do to you, maybe clap you in irons until we dock in Kingston and leave you there when we sail. I'll be honest with you, Nate, we've got us a bad situation on this ship. Furtado's as much master of her as the Captain. And don't ask me how or why. As for our real cargo, we'll take it on in Kingston and if talk around the scuttlebutt talk is true, deliver it to Vera Cruz. But what it is I don't know and I don't care. I just keep my mouth shut, and I advise you to do the same."

I said no more openly about the cargo and my thoughts were distracted days later by the sights, colors, and sounds of Kingston, but above all by the people. I had almost no experience with Africans, having seen a few Blacks, usually from afar, working the Virginia fields. I was rendered slack jawed by the cadence of their songs and agile rhythmic movements. Unlike the grave demeanor of my Cherokee relatives and the discordant gestures of my white kinsmen, the Blacks seemed to me to do everything with an effortless sinuosity. Nor was it the special talent of a few. They all seemed attuned to a spontaneous rhythm of movement and sound that they all unerringly sensed by some mysterious instinct imperceptible to other races. As far as I could tell, only the very old Blacks seemed to lose the African rhythm. But then I have observed that in old age all people leave behind most of their differences and sink to a lower, common level in appearance and attitude. Toward the end of their life once bitter enemies have only affection or indifference for their former adversaries. The very young play in harmony and the very old live in peace. It is in their middle years of greatest strength and ambition when men fight and kill one another under the prod of great lusts and strong causes. Why is it that when men are strong they are most prone to wrong? I have no answer to my question and make no claim to any particular insight. It is only as I grow older that I reflect at all on such trifling matters. In youth I was more impressed by what I saw than what I thought.

What I saw in Kingston impressed me overmuch. Before I realized what was happening, the African drums and rhythms had so hypnotized me and drink had done the rest that I lost consciousness. Mason and other sailors mockingly told me that they had to drag me back to ship. When I came to my senses, I felt the swaying motion of the vessel and the shuddering of strong wind in the sails. But of purse and money I had none. God knows what furtive black hands—male or female—had made away with my modest funds.

"Let it be a lesson to you, lad," laughed Mason. "Next time it could be a slit throat or a dagger in the belly. The Blacks will bow and call you 'Massa' and 'Governah', but they will rob and kill you for your valuables as readily as the common footpads of London or New York. And like all subservient people, they are usually cleverer than their masters about such things."

"What of our cargo?" I asked.

"The Black stevedores took it on board while you were drunk and the rest of the crew were amusing themselves with the girls."

"And what was the cargo?"

"As I told you before, it's best not to ask. All I can say is that New Spain, or Mexico as they are calling it now, has risen in revolt against Spain, and I suspect that our cargo has something to do with the war. The Captain and Mate kept us in the dark. That's why they wanted all hands off the vessel last night."

In contrast to Kingston, if you ask me about Vera Cruz I will tell you that I never saw the city. With trimmed sail the *Chesapeake* made her way slowly up the deserted New Spain coastline. All I could see of human presence was smoke rising above palm fronds. Whereupon we dropped anchor and Furtado or one of his men signaled with a mirror. Soon a large boat emerged from the tropical foliage and came toward us.

Furtado's followers had trundled ten sealed crates on deck as we looked on under the Captain's orders to stand clear of the transaction. "Guns and ammunitions I'm guessing," mused Mason, and the men around us nodded in nervous agreement.

"If that's so," said ship cook Hiram Benson, nervously rubbing his gray chin whiskers, "the sooner we get out of here, the better our chances will be. This ship is swift, but my brother's been to Tampico, which is not far north of here, and he tells me the Spanish have a garrison there with naval support. As defenseless as we are, a broadside or two from one of the two San Ildefonso class battleships my brother saw there would send us to the bottom. And even if some of us survived and made it to shore, they would execute us for aiding the revolutionaries."

Benson's words quickly turned prophetic. Barely had the boat come within hailing distance than a sail cleared a promontory on the northern horizon and a vessel came into full view. "A San Ildefonso warship!" yelled the sharp-eyed Captain Johnson. "All hands to posts! Weigh anchor! Step lively!"

The Spanish vessel was at full sail and closing rapidly as our crew weighed anchor and scrambled to set our sails for full running speed. At that moment we saw a puff of smoke and then heard a distant detonation. The cannon ball came nowhere near our vessel and instantly we saw that it was not meant for us, but for the boat. The first ball fell harmlessly in the water, but a second caused the boat to rise from the waves, spilling crew members. We could see them flailing in the choppy sea only to disappear one by one as the ship hove within musket range to dispatch the unfortunate wretches.

Another cannonade then sounded but passed over our prow and splashed harmlessly in the water a hundred yards ahead of us. It was understood as an order to drop anchor and await the warship. Naturally, Captain Johnson had no intention of obeying. The *Chesapeake* swung smartly around in response to Furtado's expert seamanship, and as the full deployment of sails filled and strained in a good wind, we surged southward.

Meanwhile the warship was pulling within cannon range of

the *Chesapeake*. Training his spyglass on it, Captain Johnson told Bosun Adkins in a low but emotional voice that it was the *Asia 64*. Commissioned in 1789 with 74 cannon but now modified to carry 80.

"I know the ship and if Alberto Moreno still captains her, we face an experienced seaman who neither gives quarter nor asks it. If he gets within range, he'll make splinters and spars of our vessel and rags of our sails! Get down there with Hurtado and do everything you can to get us more sail! We are doomed if we cannot outrun her!"

A sailor working with the cables overheard the conversation and spread the word. We were petrified by panic. And with good cause; despite a gallant effort, the flying *Chesapeake* could not escape entirely our pursuer's early favorable momentum and fell briefly within cannon range of the *Asia 64*. Fifteen or twenty of its cannon fired on us. Most of the balls fell harmlessly into the water, for we were now too far ahead for consistent accuracy. But two found their mark amidships and by ill luck carried away Captain Johnson, Bosun Adkins, and Hank Filmore, the sailor working with the tangled cables.

There was no time to waste. Durward Mason yelled for me to follow him to assess the damage. It was even worse than we dreaded. Water was pouring through two breaches in the hull and quickly rising in the hold.

"Quick, Nathan," yelled Durward, "nail the timbers lengthwise across the two breaks! They're close enough together to cover with a single double-ply set of braces! Then we can reinforce them with crossing vertical boards!"

Though still with only partial mastery of ship carpentry, I remembered some techniques that Master Oglivie taught me and reasoned that the patchwork that Durward intended would be too weak to stand the turbulence and pressure and might instead cause the whole section to tear loose and sink the ship.

"Your pardon, but I don't recommend it, Mr. Mason. If it doesn't hold then that section of the hull will break loose and we'll be under water in a matter of minutes."

"So what would you, sir, with your long experience, recommend?" he asked sarcastically.

"Two things: first, we have timbers and oakum, and metal sheeting wide enough by my calculations to go from rib to rib. After we put wedges in the breaches along with all the oakum we can push in around them, we will need to lay on double layers of the metal sheeting and secure each end to the ribs with iron bolts and, second, reinforce it with all with the best timbers we have, and not just the area around the breaches but that whole side of the hull. That way I think it will hold so that we can pump out enough water to get to the nearest port outside of Spanish waters. All that provided the Spaniards don't overtake us and finish the destruction."

Durward started to object, but thought better of it and muttered grudgingly: "It might work."

Durward naturally resented my youthfulness, but he was wise enough to see the advantage of my strategy. He yelled for two men to come down to help us. With their help on the pump and the oakum, in thirty minutes we had the worst leaks stanched to a controllable degree. If all went according to plan, the leakage would diminish as the wood swelled and compressed the oakum. Everything depended on the integrity of the hull. But if it was not further compromised we had a chance to save the vessel and ourselves.

During all this time we were ignorant of the pursuit. When finally our repairs were done and I was able to go on deck to get water and inquire about our situation, I learned that despite her wounds, the *Chesapeake* had safely raced ahead of the ponderous *Asia 64*. But instead of elation, the mood of the crewmen was subdued because of the loss of Captain Johnson and their shipmates.

We all assumed, at least the crewmen I talked with, that Furtado would put us into port at Kingston in order to make more substantial repairs than our patchwork measures at sea. But Furtado, others cautiously advised us, had his reasons for avoiding Kingston.

I knew little about life and law on the high seas, but enough to be aware that the death of a ship captain was a serious business that would require a formal inquiry. Add to this important circumstance the ominous fact that his death occurred far from the announced destination of the *Chesapeake*. Naturally, this would raise suspicions of mutiny, piracy, or contraband that once spread abroad could implicate us all. As for Furtado himself, those who disliked the man hinted that he had a turbid and perhaps criminal past, though they revealed no details to me.

For three days we limped along the north coast of Cuba, giving a wide berth to Havana, which was certain to have Spanish vessels in port. Even more fearful were the British warships on the lookout for slave runners bringing human cargo to work and die in the sugarcane fields of "the Pearl of the Antilles". Some of the English captains had a habit, I was told, of shooting first and asking questions later.

Here I cannot pretend a courage that was completely lacking

in me at the time. I was terrified that the combination of a long voyage in rough seas infamous for sudden gales and destructive winds would overwhelm our repairs and sink us, for I knew better than anyone aboard how flimsy they were. Surely, I reasoned, we would have to put into a port, but where that would be no one could tell me, and for reasons that only later became clear, Furtado and his henchmen seemed recklessly indifferent to the fate of the *Chesapeake*.

A nightfall later found us almost becalmed but drifting with drooped sails close to the Cuban reefs some miles from a place called Cruz del Padre. Now seasoned sailors amongst us were also becoming alarmed. Our fears were soon justified as the swift tropical night descended. There was a sudden scraping noise, followed by a crunching shudder and a pop of snapping timbers, as the *Chesapeake*, pierced and pivoting on an up-thrusted pointed rock, swayed to a scant four feet of water in the shallow reef.

Furtado ordered us ashore. But we soon discovered the folly of his command. Mosquitoes descended on us like a biblical pestilence. The men screamed curses and beat futilely with rags and branches. It occurred to me that I could escape the torment by burying myself in the sand and covering my head with a shirt. Some of the men tried to go back to our stranded vessel, but Furtado would have none of it. Then seeing the measures I was taking to protect myself, most also tried the ploy.

Durward Mason, his exasperation with me finally overcoming his good sense, declined. Instead, he preferred to immerse himself in the water and cover his head with a shirt like the rest of us. Hiram Benson cautioned him.

"Durward, I wouldn't stay down there in the water if I was

you. There's sharks and caimans, they call them, along these shores and danger aplenty for all of us here. Why don't you come up here and dig under the sand like the rest of us? I had my scullion Pete slip out a couple of muskets and some spare blankets I keep in the scullery. It's better if we stick together."

"I'll be just fine," Durward said testily. "I know a thing or two and can take care of myself. You just go along there with Mr. Stokes. He seems to know everything except how to wipe his butt and keep his mouth shut."

Hiram sighed and shook his head. "That cussed stubborn streak will be the death of him yet."

And in a way it was. We never saw Durward again, although the next day a piece of his shirt was floating close to the *Chesapeake*. At first we thought he had slipped back on board and had not thought to look for him, but later when it was apparent that Durward was nowhere to be found, Benson described his probable demise.

"Caiman musta got him. I tried to tell the damn fool, but he wouldn't listen. He's probably out there somewhere on the bottom. The big caimans and crocs—and gators up in Florida they say—will grab a grown man, pull him under water, and then spin him till he's good and dead. Later, when they get hungry, they'll come back and eat their kill, one chunk at a time. To them we're just another piece of meat, and they like it better half rotten than fresh."

"You sure about that?" asked Porter Foreman, "I thought these Cuban caimans didn't bother people."

"I guess somebody forgot to tell that to the caimans, didn't they?" said Benson. "When they get hungry enough they'll go after anything that moves, man or beast. And they say these

Cuban caimans can jump up and grab birds and animals in low hanging tree limbs."

"Leastwise, we won't have to bother with burying him," laughed Milford Tapscot.

"Before all this is over, Tapscot," scolded Benson, "you may be hoping there are still some of us left to say words over your own carcass."

"You could be right," Tapscot answered in a subdued tone. "But tell me, do you know something you're not telling us?"

"No, I don't, Tapscot, and you can stop your questions right there. I don't know any more than the rest of you. It's just a feeling I get about Furtado's bunch of cutthroats. They're two-legged versions of that caiman that drug old Durward to his death."

"Well, I have one question I've been mulling over that I'm going to ask all of you anyway," Tapscot said, "and I don't give a damn what you say, Benson. Why did Furtado order us off the vessel and into this hellish jungle?"

"What are you thinking, Tapscot?" asked Foreman.

"If what I'm thinking is about to happen, I'm for striking out for the interior. I don't like Spaniards and they sure as hell don't like us, but I think we'd have a better chance with them than with Furtado's bunch. On that point, I'm with Benson. I'm getting a bad feeling about all this."

"But what is it?" asked Foreman. "Furtado's gonna need us to get the ship off that rock on the sandbar. He can't do it with just the five or six that follow him."

"Maybe he's got more men on the way."

"More?" laughed Benson. "Look around, Tapscot, this place is deserted."

"Well, I don't know about that. The other day I heard them talking Portuguese, and while I don't understand the language, it's a lot like Spanish that I know a little. They stopped talking when they saw me, which is a little suspicious in itself, but they were saying things like '*chegada*' and I think I heard something like '*nossa outra tripulacao*. I got to thinking about it, putting two and two together, and I believe it means 'arrival' and 'our other crew'. I'm not saying it does, because all I know is a little Spanish, and the words may not match and mean what I think. But, men, the more I think about it, the more I believe we're in one hell of a dangerous situation."

"Meaning what?" asked Benson, suddenly taking Tapscot's fears very seriously.

"Meaning that Furtado may have another ship and crew on the way here, and if he does, we could either be abandoned to starve in this godforsaken place, or, possibly shot on the spot. Furtado has all the guns and ammo we were supposed to deliver to the revolutionaries, and we're sitting here covered with mosquitoes, no food, and with only a couple of old muskets."

"But how could he have set up such a scheme? I can't imagine Captain Johnson being involved in anything like you're talking about," said Benson.

"Maybe he wasn't, but he was willing to run contraband to the Mexican rebels, wasn't he? Anyway, he was only one man, and Furtado could have killed him when the time came. This may be something Furtado has been planning for a long time, even before we left Salem."

"Or maybe it's your imagination running wild, Milford. Why don't we wait and see if this mysterious crew shows up before we run off half-cocked into wild country we know nothing about? Even if we made contact with Spanish officials, they would arrest us on whatever charges they please."

"True, true," admitted Tapscot. I say wait to see what happens but be ready to run inland if they show up."

Meanwhile, to my surprise I was summoned on board. "Mr. Furtado wants you to start working on the repairs," a gaunt Brazilian by the name of Lenheiro explained. And he wants you to find Mason and bring him along."

"We think Mason is dead. Caimans got him last night."

Lenheiro shrugged his shoulders dismissively. "Then you are now our carpenter. Furtado was going to name you so anyway."

Upon inspection, I saw that the massive rip in the *Chesapeake*'s hull was beyond our capability to repair. I told Furtado so.

"Don't worry. This vessel is not going anywhere. Help is on the way and soon we shall be gone from this miserable place."

His words all but confirmed the fears of my crewmates. I said nothing to Furtado or the other sailors, but to myself, I vowed, if possible, to alert my stranded companions. I asked permission to go ashore to retrieve my shirt, but Furtado, suddenly suspicious, refused. Later he sent Lenheiro and another man ashore armed with muskets. I heard a shot but within the hour they returned emptyhanded.

Reasoning among themselves, our stranded shipmates must have concluded that summoning me aboard meant that my services as ship's carpenter would be needed and theirs would not. In any case, my companions waited no longer; evidently they had decided to strike out for the interior. The next day there was no sign that any remained on the sandy beach.

I never saw any of them again and must leave their story unfinished. I wondered if they died of starvation in the wilderness or made contact with a Spanish outpost or patrol. I feared that if any among them was careless enough to let slip intelligence of our clandestine voyage to Vera Cruz, then the lives of all would be in danger. The Spanish would be within legal rights to condemn them as piratical *filibusteros* and execute them by firing squad or hanging. And the same would be true for the entire crew of the *Chesapeake*, myself included. When the full realization of the danger struck me, I went from dreading the arrival of another vessel to hoping it would show up quickly and remove us from Spanish territory.

In this hope I was not disappointed. Late that same afternoon a dashing, arrow-shaped ship known in Caribbean waters as a "slaver" hove into view under a Portuguese flag. But since the Spanish distrusted the Portuguese as much as they detested British, French and American freebooters, we were hardly better off than before.

Furtado knew far better than I how perilous our circumstances were. For unbeknownst to me, the craft had been purchased and refitted at the Casa Blanca of Havana and cleared for the Madeira Islands. The latter ploy deceived no one, least of all the Spanish officials versed in the all tricks of the illicit slave trade. But they were willing, for a price, to turn a blind eye long enough for the vessel to clear the Morro channel. After that, it was up to the *Dourada*, as it was renamed, to fend for itself against patrolling English warships in open waters.

Furtado wasted no time in ordering the crew to transfer the cargo of guns, powder, ammunition, timbers, cables, stores, water, tools, and anything else of use and value from the stricken *Chesapeake* to the sleek *Dourada*. When this was done to his satisfaction, he gave a signal to an expert swimmer remaining on the *Chesapeake* to torch it in several places and quickly come on board. By the time we stood two miles off the Cuban coastline the *Chesapeake* lit up the dark skies with its spectacular funeral pyre.

The next day I marveled at the lines and workmanship of the *Dourada*. At forty-five tons with a culverine amidships and the trim, rakish dimensions mentioned previously, it seemed to my carpenter's eye a thing of high craft and beauty. On the other hand, the requisites for the transport of slaves puzzled and disturbed me. I could hardly imagine how human beings could survive in conditions that by my measurements allowed almost no movement or personal space. But since it was all still vaguely abstract and untested by real experience on my part, I put it out of my mind and paid attention to practical matters as ship's carpenter.

Four days out a gale roiled the seas and the waves rose to monstrous size. But for all his human faults, Furtado was an excellent seaman. Some of crew grumbled in fear when he ordered up more canvas, for they were hoping instead that he would bring down the foresail and turn the vessel to the wind with bare masts. Instead, Furtado chose to match sail with sea and so sent the *Dourada* scudding mightily through the storm until by noon of the following morning both sea and human spirits were again placid. Afterwards, no one questioned Furtado's orders or doubted his seamanship.

CHAPTER 4

Without other incidents worthy of recounting, thirty-nine days later with favorable tide and wind, we ended our voyage at the mouth of the Rio Pongo south of the great bulge of West Africa and hard by the squalid river settlement of Bangalang and its *barracoons*, or slave pens. I found myself in a world magnificent and savage beyond anything I knew or could have imagined. And beautiful? I am tempted to add it to my impressions, except that it is too soft and dainty a word to describe what I saw of Africa.

It had become known to me to my great surprise that Furtado's daughter Catherine was married to Englishman Reginald Brighton, who claimed de facto lordship of the Pongo and costal territories extending inland to the lower reaches of the Mandingo kingdom.

Furtado was disturbed and angered on three counts: first, he could not understand why his daughter had accompanied her husband on what, at a formal level, Americans or Europeans would call a state visit to the Mandingo ruler, who annually sent hundreds of "Bush Blacks" to Brighton's barracoons. The visit was an extraordinary event. Seldom did whites—and never white women—venture inland, especially this close to the rainy season. But lately word got out that the Mandingo King Ben Ibrahim was secretly negotiating with French slavers and considering sending his annual roundup of slaves to their factories down the coast. Gifts and guile were quickly needed on a vast scale to avert the catastrophe, and the wily Brighton was best suited to the task. A meeting was arranged on the loosely defined border between the costal territories and the Mandingo Empire.

Second, Furtado was distressed to see that Brighton's *barracoons* were less than a third full of serviceable slaves, though another score of old, useless Blacks had been released to save food. These were too spent to make their way back to their inland homeland. Instead, they shambled about Bangalang, begging and enduring kicks and insults by the exasperated villagers, black and white.

Third, Brighton's house guards inexplicably denied Furtado and his officers lodging in the "Big House," as it was called, forcing the Portuguese Captain and our entire crew to sleep aboard the *Dourada*. Furtado was in a murderous mood but the guards were adamant and uncharacteristically tightlipped. Short of storming the residence, there was nothing to do but wait until Brighton's return with wife Catherine and the news, so it was hoped, that negotiations had been successfully concluded and the Mandingos would soon be driving hordes of new slaves—the currency of Black Africa—coastward.

That very night, however, every assumption and perspective changed. A young Spaniard named Miguel Astorga, in Brighton's employ as secretary and factotum, asked and received permission to come aboard the *Dourada*. There he told a horrifying story of betrayal. Brighton, he explained to Furtado, having succumbed to the lax African customs concerning marriage, had abandoned his Christian heritage and taken multiple Black wives since his marriage to Catherine. The closely guarded harem in the Big House accounted for the refusal to offer accommodations to Furtado and his officers. But the worst part, Astorga said, unable to hold back his tears, was that Catherine herself was the prize that Brighton offered King Ben Ibrahim in exchange for a new pact. And given the sexual lust of African despots for young European women, she would be a gift the King could not refuse. Thus it was expected that an agreement would be reached and new slaves would be herded into the *barracoons*. As for Brighton, once rid of Catherine's daily screams of protest, could settle into the indolent life of a petty African despot. On the other hand, Catherine herself, Astorga said despairingly, would be the target of unthinkable cruelties inflicted not by the King but by the jealous and vengeful Black wives in his seraglio, to say nothing of being forced to foreswear Christianity and convert to Islam.

"Unless she is rescued quickly, don Manuel," he added tearfully, "your daughter will have a short and painful life without friends or protectors."

Instead of ranting and cursing, as we all expected him to do, Furtado grew strangely silent and his face was expressionless, save for his eyes that flashed with mountainous passions.

"And you, young Miguel," he asked after a pause, "did you have a part in arranging Brighton's atrocity? And why do you tell me this about my daughter? What do you want from me?"

"Sir, I could not stoop so low as to betray my condition as a Christian and a man. I had nothing to do with Brighton's treachery, and my only concern is Catherine's welfare and happiness. I will offer my life for her if I can help rescue her from the horrors that await her and may have commenced already."

"What, then, are your feelings for my daughter?"

"Sir, I shall not withhold from you that I have loved her in silence since you brought her to Bangalang two years ago to marry Brighton. And though she has never said so in words, I believe she would love me if she could. As far as circumstances permitted, I have been her friend throughout."

"Then she shall be your wife if we live and accomplish two things: first, kill Brighton for his villainy and, second, rescue her from the Mandingo King. Now tell me, are there other men in Bangalang that we can enlist to help us?"

"Only two that have my complete confidence, an Englishman named Michael Brownley, who holds grudges against Brighton for several wrongs done him, and my cousin, Primitivo Astorga, who is unconditionally loyal to me."

"Then collect them at once and bring them here so that we may plan our strategy. Know you the country well enough to lead us to the Mandingo encampment?"

"Not I, I have been no more than a league upriver in my three years here, but the English hunter knows the country far and wide, all the way into the Mandingo highland."

Within the hour Astorga returned with his kinsman Primitivo, a short but strongly muscled Castilian of twenty-five, and Brownley, a rangy, blond-bearded Londoner above thirty-five. Both pledged to aid our band in any way they could.

"We must move quickly," Furtado said to our motley band of twenty-four. "The Mandingo, though somewhat civilized in the Muslim way and considered the aristocracy of Black Africa, love long festivals and music as much as the bush Blacks under their dominion. So it is likely they will celebrate for a week before beginning their return journey. And if I know anything about the Mandingo, courtesy demands that Brighton remain until the festivities are over. If we can take them by surprise before they withdraw out of our reach, we may rout and scatter the lot of them. So dreaded are the Mandingo by the savage tribes around them that they fear no attack and take few precautions. A single Mandingo warrior can inspire panic in a whole band of the bush people. But if this is a sign of their strength, it may also prove to be their weakness. And we shall exploit it in a way they will not soon forget. Now, tell me, Mr. Brownley, where and how shall we find their camp?"

"No doubt Brighton met them at their accustomed lowland post where they customarily deal with whites. And for a transaction of this magnitude the King himself, not one of his princes, will be present. If my supposition is correct they will not yet have decamped, even if an agreement has been reached in principle. The Mandingo are a people of much formality and ceremony in all their affairs and scrupulous in obeying all the precepts of their religion. They know that whites are an impatient people and for this reason prolong their negotiations with them to an extreme in order to gain advantage. They regard haste as both a sign of weakness and an unpardonable breach of ethics, and have a secret scorn of whites because of it. As for the camp, it lies in the foothills of the Fouta Djallon Mountains at a three-day journey, two by river and another by land. The place is purely ceremonial and unfortified, and usually uninhabited, unlike their strongholds beyond the mountains. If we are act boldly, we can take it."

Furtado nodded and repeated, "We can take it," then added, "We must, and we leave at first light to do so."

Supplied with enough guns, ammunition from our undelivered contraband stock to arm a troop thrice our size— we loaded ourselves into three capacious boats, leaving room for food and water. Obvious to all, but commented by none, Miguel Astorga prepared a special curtained space for Catherine. I knew, as I think we all did, by the grim set of his features that he would not return alive without her.

For a moment his anguish and my melancholy memories of Jane Olgivie merged in a wrenching conviction of life's futility. What was I doing? Why was I here? What was the meaning of this or of anything, for that matter? At that instant I had the horrifying feeling that my life was not only pointless but might soon be over before I had a chance to live it. I was grateful that Hurtado, displeased with my momentary idleness in the midst of our frantic preparations, sharply ordered me to be alert and busy myself with the loading.

As our boats pushed off upstream, the jungle protested with the raucous cries of hidden birds and shrill screams of monkeys that mocked our desire for stealth and silence. The night with its duels of death and devouring was lifting and nature was conducting its indifferent morning requiem for the slaughtered. I struggled in vain to recall my hereditary Cherokee understanding of nature. It was no use; there was no match. I had grown up in a gentler nature, a creation of the kinder climes of earth's higher latitudes.

We proceeded apace, now used to the jungle cries but molested occasionally by monstrous bugs and hungry mosquitoes and alert to motionless crocodiles watching us from the banks or eyeing us like submerged logs in the narrowing river.

After two days the Pongo had shrunk to the size of a wide American creek. The jungle was now sporadically interspersed with broad stretches of attractive grassland. At an unmarked spot known only to Brownley, he instructed us that it was time to leave the river and strike out overland. We took great pains to conceal the boats and cover the extra supplies with heavy canvas.

Furtado and Astorga were of a mind to push on at once, but Brownley cautioned them that we must rest and take sustenance so as to be at full strength for the assault. "Besides, now that we are leaving the jungle and entering the savannah, we may encounter big cats ahead."

We heeded Brownley's advice and camped near the boats. The next day, we saw nothing of the great felines but were roused to alertness several times in the night by their roars. The next day around noon we began to hear the steady, unnerving throb of tom-toms.

"We are now six to eight miles from the encampment," Brownley told us. "From here on we must be doubly vigilant. The Mandingo themselves do not often venture into the jungle or the grasslands, but their slave scouts keep them informed."

"You did not tell us this before," Furtado chided him.

"If we considered every possible danger beforehand, Captain, we might be too discouraged to take the first step. There are always perils we cannot foresee, and some we know of are best left uncommented. I have lived in Africa long enough to believe that spoken words often summon the things we fear."

Furtado nodded. "I cannot disagree, Mr. Brownley, so lead the way. I will brave the jaws of Hell itself for my daughter."

We had not gone a mile further when a painted warrior rose from the high grass, screaming and brandishing a lance. Astorga raised his rifle, but Brownley pushed the barrel aside with his left hand and with his right let fly a twelve-inch steel knife. The weapon whistled and buried itself in the man's back as he turned to flee.

"A Nalu," said Brownley, turning the corpse over to look at the face and body markings. "They do not usually range this far south of their homeland. The Mandingo must be expanding their empire."

"Search the area widely and carefully," Furtado ordered several of his men, "but if you find other scouts, use your knives if possible. And fire your weapons only as a last resort. Our whole strategy depends on stealth and ambush."

Now doubly cautious, we advanced slowly toward the camp. The tom-toms grew louder and before long we perceived distant music and faint voices.

"What is your advice now, Mr. Brownley?" asked Furtado. We are here and in place for the assault. What say you? Where is Catherine most likely to be?"

"You can see the central tent, larger than the others. In it all the principals of the festivities will be congregated, including most assuredly your daughter, Brighton and the Mandingo leaders, perhaps the King himself. The Mandingo protocol does not vary. There we must strike, suddenly and lethally. This is no time for sentimentalities about sparing human life. Only your daughter matters. There is no reason to delay. Are you then ready and does everyone understand the plan?"

"We are ready and on my count of three we rush the tent, killing all in our path: one, two, three!"

We rose as one and screaming pent-up cries of death and defiance rushed the compound, firing as we went. For an instant, the human tableau was frozen in utter stupefaction and bewilderment, then scattered in terror before our charge. In a thrice ten valiant Mandingo warriors died with spears in hand. The less courageous fled with two of the Mandingo princes. We never saw the King or knew what became of him, but supposed that he was spirited away to safety by his guards. Three of Brighton's white guards closed protectively around him, but they fell under our withering fire. Brighton himself was down from a bullet but conscious and trying to crawl through his own blood to safety. Furtado checked him with a saber to his stomach.

"I will not waste words with you, for we have other killing to do. But this is in payment for your treachery!"

So saying, he drove the saber through Brighton's stomach and left him to lie and die.

Meanwhile, as the killing and screaming continued among the Blacks, Miguel came from behind a curtained area, escorting the terrified and trembling Catherine. One of the braver Mandingo warriors, witnessing the outrage of a Christian touching a consecrated Muslim bride to be of the King himself, rushed to defend her. But Primitivo felled him with a single shot.

In less than five minutes the carnage ended with all the assembly either dead or fled. Forty Mandingo warriors and nobles and eight whites, including Brighton, had fallen in the onslaught. Of our men, two had been cornered and hacked to death by the bravest Mandingo warriors. But Catherine, the object of our raid, was alive, if not exactly well, and only death itself could have removed Miguel Astorga from her side.

Now our circumstances were reversed and perilously magnified. Without the element of surprise, we faced the prospect of having to fight our way step by step back to the Pongo pursued by the King's fanatical warriors, outraged by the surprise attack.

"We must march all night," said Brownley, "before they can gather their warriors and allies. We are doomed if we cannot reach our boats or if the Mandingo or their allies should happen to discover them first."

"Our advantage," observed Furtado, "is that we have superior arms and a head start. And best of all, we have Catherine. So let the race begin."

"Catherine is a precious prize to us, but her rescue is a consuming shame for the Mandingo," said Brownley. "When word spreads that we have snatched her away under the very noses of the Mandingo, they will be mad for revenge. For if they cannot punish us, their prestige among conquered and allied peoples will suffer. Black Africans are quick to abandon sworn loyalties and servitude if they perceive a loss of strength in their masters."

"Is it not the same with all people?" wondered Furtado. "But we waste time in idle talk. Let us move out while there is still daylight. And God has favored us with a full moon tonight."

Both Miguel and Manuel Furtado were worried that Catherine appeared to be in a stupor. But compliantly she marched as her father ordered, occasionally stopping to rest but saying nothing to their solicitous entreaties. Her condition slowed our progress, but by midmorning the next day, we espied the Pongo ahead—and awaiting us, a mixed troop of Mandingo and their allies.

We did not await their attack, but as we had done at the encampment charged toward the main body, shooting as we went. Against the the superiority of our weapons and ample supply of ammunition, their primitive arms could not prevail. The concentration of men on the river, which at first appeared to be to their advantage, soon turned into their second downfall. As our firepower mowed down their forces, the survivors had nowhere to run and many were gunned down as they fled laterally upriver. Three of our men were wounded by a sprinkling of ancient French muskets, but their wounds appeared to be—and so it turned out—healable.

Either the Mandingo had discovered and destroyed one of our boats, or it had sunk for other reasons, taking food and supplies to the bottom. But two proved to be sufficiently water-worthy to get us back to Bangalang. We arrived tired, triumphant, and speaking for myself, glad to be alive.

Although our men were exhausted, Furtado and Brownley posted a watch. But the night passed peacefully. The next morning they gathered our troop for a council on the fate of Bangalang. We noted with relief that Catherine, who had rested in her father's quarters aboard the *Dourada*, appeared much more alert to people and her surroundings.

"The first order of business for us," said Furtado, "should be the dismissal of Brighton's women and remaining guards. But the fate of Bangalang is not my affair."

"If it please you, Captain," offered Brownley, "I believe I can direct things here with a few trusted men until the British patrol pays its scheduled visit."

"And what will you say to them about what has transpired in our time here?"

"The truth, but perhaps not all the details," laughed Brownley. Bangalang has outlived its time and usefulness, if ever it had any. I, for one, would like to see the *barracoons* closed and the human trafficking stopped. In this regard, I am in agreement with the will and actions of the English Parliament."

"Then the place is yours to do with it as you see fit. But I came here for slaves," Furtado asserted, "and I do not intend to leave without them."

"Then with misgivings I say take aboard your vessel the sixty-odd poor devils that remain and be on your way to Cuba or Brazil or wherever you will. And keep your specie, or whatever you intended to use as payment. After the *barracoons* are emptied I intend to close and burn them."

"And what will you do with yourself afterwards, Mr. Brownley?" asked Miguel.

"I have no clearly formed idea, Miguel, only that I have been in Africa long enough, maybe too long. Perhaps I shall return to old England after all these years, or try my luck in America or Australia. I am still young enough to make a new start. These past days have reminded of something I had forgot: this is not my land."

"You may sail with us if you are of a mind to leave this place," said Furtado. "We head first to Brazil with our cargo. It is also a great land for fresh starts. But from there you may go where you will."

"Father, may I say something?" said Catherine to our great surprise and delight. For she had said nothing audible since her rescue.

"Of course, my dear, say on."

"Miguel and I have talked, and he has confessed to me his feelings. My recent ordeals weigh too dreadfully on me to make decisions of any sort, especially sentimental ones. But…"

"But what, dear Catherine?" Furtado asked with a gentleness we had not seen in him before.

"When things return to normal, if ever they do, he will be foremost in my life. We hope to start a new life in Brazil and that one day you and his cousin Primitivo will join us there."

"I understand and have given Miguel my permission to marry you in due time. But what is your point?"

"Only that you, father, treat Mr. Brownley and the other men with honor. I know they helped gain my freedom at the risk of their own lives, and I shall always be grateful to them for it."

"As shall I, dear daughter. You did not need to make the request for me to keep it always."

On that happy note our meeting ended. The remaining guards were dismissed with stern warnings not to return, and the women Brighton had collected were released with instructions to return to their villages. Some loudly protested how wronged they were, as they scooped up all the clothes they could carry. Others begged recompense for their suffering and gloomy marital prospects, tearfully assuring us that their families would not take them back and no man would have them. None of the eight betrayed any remorse that I witnessed for their late husband. Brownley gave each one a handful of coins and trinkets from Brighton's collections—a double portion to two that appeared to be pregnant—which brightened their dispositions considerably.

The next morning Furtado ordered us to attach interlinked ankle chains to all the able-bodied slaves, sixty-two in number, and herd them aboard the *Dourada*. They whimpered in wide-eyed terror, imploring us in their several tongues, which I could not understand but supposed from their tears and the tone of their voice, to be merciful. It was not from dread of slavery, Brownley told us, which all understood as a normal human condition in the world they knew, but in fear of boarding the ship, which they believed would drop them to their death in the ocean.

"That myth started decades ago," he explained, "when a ship under a Captain Daniel Stafford foundered near here and some of the slaves made it back to land. Since then they look on all slavers as murderers. And in a sense, they are not far wrong, are they?"

The next day, after taking on water, wood, and what supplies were still available, we bade farewell to Brownley, weighed anchor, and hoisted sail bound for Brazil. Reluctantly, Brownley allowed us to attach one of the remaining boats to the *Dourada*. Never again did I see or have news of him, but I always remembered the blond-bearded Englishman kindly. An hour later we saw smoke rising from Bangalang. We surmised that Brownley had made good on his promise to burn the *barracoons*, and we, for the second time, marked our departure with a fiery conflagration.

For twenty-five days all went well. Having overcome their fears of being dropped into the water, the slaves, most of whom were young and strong, had settled into a peaceful docility. Because they were fewer than the vessel was equipped to accommodate they were more comfortable and almost free of the infections and diseases that traditionally condemned many to death before they reached the Americas. On Furtado's orders, the slaves were put to work cleaning their deck of human filth. And also following his orders, we obliged them to strip and bathe every two days in a huge vat or tub brought out on deck for that purpose. At first, the sight of the bare-breasted females unnerved me, but since the uncommon often seen soon becomes commonplace, so it was with me. By our navigator Joaquim Pessoa's calculations in another week approximately the *Dourada* would be approaching the friendly port of Recife on the great Brazilian bulge. We had not seen a single British warship in the crossing and already we were beginning to breathe easier and feel festive.

But our celebration began too soon. The next day at six bells a sleepy crewman coming off his morning watch spotted what appeared to be a squall line coming rapidly at us from the east. He ran to alert Furtado who made his customary decision to run in full sailing regalia before it. But this time his luck—and ours—ran out. It was no ordinary squall but a hurricane ranging well south of the normal Atlantic storm track. Mountainous waves soon rose, swamping the slender *Dourada*, and before other maneuvers could be tried she was reduced in a half hour to a helpless derelict. Both masts snapped low in the shrieking wind and fell in full canvas and cable, one amidships, the other cleanly into the water, dragging cables and at least one man, maybe more, with it. Faintly, above the whistling din of the storm, I could hear the slaves screaming. One second I saw a dozen men running and yelling across the upheaving deck, the next they were all carried away as a monstrous wave swept it clean. Before the next arrived, on an impulse that I did not fully understand, I ran and unlocked the slave deck with a key I had devised, for Hurtado kept the master. Then the next wave, twin to its killer predecessor, struck and carried me with it. I hit the water headfirst and plunged so deep that I counted my life as finished. But then with bursting lungs I was thrown in a somersault into the air long enough to draw new breath and prolong my fragile lease on life. Up and down the water tossed me, draining me of sense and strength. Then I came down a final time and my hand struck a solid object. It was a broken timber from the dying *Dourada*. I clung to it with the last strength I could muster and watched the vessel describe a mad pirouette, whirling ever faster as it stood almost perpendicular to the water before sliding into the depths. I caught sight of a few bobbing black bodies and shipmates circling the sinking ship. For a terrifying moment the sucking vortex created by its demise threatened to pull me down with it. But then the funnel closed and the debris scattered at the mercy of other forces. The rain was now became so dense that I could see nothing.

CHAPTER 5

For what must have been several hours I drifted in stunned semi-consciousness, nauseous from exhaustion and the salt water I had swallowed. But my arms remained locked in a death grip around the spar.

When things began to come back into focus I found myself bobbing within swimming distance of a low shoreline and kicked off towards it, pushing the timber before me. The Brazilian coast! I thought with rising hope.

But no; later I discovered I was on a bank or island of limited dimensions, as best I could make out in the uncertain light and low-flying clouds, perhaps a mile in irregular circumference and rising to a modest peak near its center. The windswept eastern slope where I had come aground in ankle deep mud was almost bare of vegetation, but later as I made my way just past the central hill I espied palm trees and a profusion of other trees and shrubs surrounding a lone manmade structure. There I hastened, hoping to make human contact.

In this second hope I was also disappointed. The building was an abandoned hacienda of the Spanish or Portuguese style, and from the looks of the few dilapidated items of furniture and rotted draperies, abandoned for many years. Water lines on the walls spoke of many floods.

None of that mattered very much to me in my condition. I had reached the limits of my endurance, and my disappointment at finding nothing of what I hoped for on the island completed my dejection. Water dripped through many holes in the broken tile roof, but there were dry areas where it still held. On one of these I piled my wet clothes and making a crude bed next to them of frayed linens and draperies, I slept uncounted hours away.

I awoke at dawn sore in body but with hunger pangs that were more bothersome. I had lost count of time, but judging from the near dryness of my clothes and the early morning sun, I calculated that I had slept close on to thirty hours. Unless, as I wondered, I had lost another day entirely. I dressed quickly but had trouble getting into my leather boots, which were shrunken and stiff. I was eager to venture outside to see whether the world into which I had fallen might contain something edible. Though food was not readily available, water was plentifully collected from the storm in clear puddles and small streams. I drank my fill, which eased my hunger a bit, then headed toward what appeared to be the remnant of an ancient orchard.

It was, but unsuited no doubt for the tropical climate and saltwater flooding, the apple and pear trees barely clung to life and bore no fruit. I saw nothing that would provide me nourishment and after circling the island, returned to the ruined hacienda frightened and despondent. Was I, then, destined to starve on this deserted island?

But I slapped my forehead for my stupidity as it suddenly occurred to me that if there was no food on the land there would be nourishment in the sea, if I could contrive a means to catch fish or other sea creatures. I searched through the house and found a rust-encrusted knife in the cupboard. I whetted it on the hard masonry and soon had a serviceable tool with which to make a wooden spear.

I fashioned a crude spear from what I thought was a species

of hardwood that resembled an ash. But spearing fish was a skill I had not yet acquired, and dozens of awkward misses discouraged me, already weak from hunger. Eventually, however, a foot-long, unnamed subject of Neptune's kingdom swam by, and even clumsier than I, became my first victim.

Now what to do with my catch? I could eat it raw, and in truth, the idea was much less repugnant than it would have been with a steady diet. On the other hand, the art of starting fires had been handed down from my Cherokee ancestors, and a cooked fish had a much great appeal than a raw one.

To sum up the matter, I started a fire with dry straw and other material in the hacienda and cooked it over the open fire, as I cooked several others in the coming days. It was a monotonous diet, and I had never especially like fish. But as a saying I learned in New England goes, "hunger makes any broth delicious."

My thoughts then turned to escaping from the island. I guessed that I was less than a hundred miles from the Brazilian mainland, stranded no doubt on one of the low-lying banks I had heard of from experienced sailors. Obviously humans had once inhabited the island but it had subsided to such dangerous levels that storms sometimes submerged it. No wonder, I thought, there appeared to be no animals except a few birds on the island.

After considering my options, I proposed to put together a raft from whatever materials and cloth I might strip from the hacienda and the few trees still standing. I still had the ship spar as a beginning. The risk was great, but the distance to the mainland was minimal. Later that morning after an auspicious breakfast of red snapper and mollusks—I was becoming more proficient as a fisherman—I began work on the raft. After finishing off the snapper for lunch, I took my knife and headed out to collect or cut what branches I could. I was in luck of sorts. The storm had torn several substantial limbs entirely from the tree trunks, while others dangled weakly. I returned, dragging my best trophies, tired but happy with my labors. But never in a million years could I have expected to see what—or better, who—was waiting for me in the hacienda.

"You!" I blurted out in astonishment. It was the red-headed gentlemen from the Boston Common comfortably resting in the only chair left in the place.

"And a good day to you, too, Nathan. Each time I see you it appears you have found some new means of distressing yourself," he chuckled in his deep baritone voice.

"How in God's name, sir, did you get here?"

"You have said it, my boy, in God's name. I am here to help you again. The way I got here does not matter, only my purpose."

"Sir, perhaps I have lost my mind. I understand none of this."

"Your mind is raw but sound enough, young man. My understanding of the matter will prove sufficient to rescue you, but only if you follow my instructions."

"I am building a raft to get to the Brazilian coast."

He held up his right hand to stop me. I noticed his gold ring with the magnificent turquoise.

"Forget the raft. You must not go there. Your salvation lies elsewhere. Besides Carib folk live along the coast, and some of them have a taste for human flesh. You are too thin and wiry to be truly delectable to them, but they would roast you nonetheless if nothing better falls into their pot."

"You, sir, guided me before. I was not able to express my gratitude then. I do so now. I thank you from the heart. Tell me what I must do."

"You will find a strip of white sail on the east beach. Attach it to a pole, one of those you are trimming, and stake it on the highest point on the island. And take care it does not fall. In a few days a whaling vessel will see it and take you aboard."

"Yes, sir. Now will you answer a question that weighs heavily on my heart?"

"You may ask."

"Many went down with our vessel. Did any besides me survive?"

"Some did. I see that your concern is mainly for Catherine and Miguel. You have no cause for grief."

"Does that mean, sir, that they and others survived the storm?"

"That is all I can tell you."

"Is there anything else I should know?"

"More than you can imagine, Nathan, more than you can imagine. But this only I shall tell you for the moment: sail no more. A survivor of three shipwrecks ought to learn to stay on land," he chuckled. Then he added with a sparkle in his blue eyes, "Your life is elsewhere. Live well and trust the Creator, as wise men say."

For the briefest instant I turned to look at a large tropical bird with brilliant red and green plumage that suddenly perched unexpectedly on the window ledge. When I turned back to my guest. He was gone, and so was the bird. I would see him once more. But that telling belongs to another time.

I followed my strange guest's instructions to the letter. The sail was where he said, and attached firmly to the pole, was soon erect atop the central hill. Three days later a whaling ship returning from the southern ocean passed by my island and dispatched a boat to fetch me aboard. I told my story in detail to Captain Braddock and the assembled crew, but the looks on several faces told me that not everyone believed me. Captain Braddock, however, was not among the skeptics. He had known Captain Johnson and had encounters with Manuel Furtado.

"Furtado was a wanted person in several countries. It is said that his backers, shadowy financiers in London seeking to profit illegally from revolutions in the Spanish American countries and slavery in Africa, supplied him capital to buy his way into partial control of the *Chesapeake*. It may be better for humanity if, indeed, he went down in Brazilian waters. In that regard, you may be asked to appear before a maritime inquest to tell what you know of Captain Johnson's fate and Furtado's activities. As far as I know, Johnson was an able seaman and it would not surprise me to learn that Furtado, not a Spanish cannon, did him in."

"I was not in any way involved in the decisions that doomed both vessels. I was obliged to serve as ship's carpenter after the man under whom I served died in Cuban waters."

"All the better to get an impartial version of what happened from someone who had no axe to grind, profits to make, or misdeeds to conceal."

"Where most likely will the inquest take place, sir?"

"Probably in Boston, but possibly in Salem."

We docked three weeks later in Boston. I thanked Captain Braddock profusely for my rescue and promised to be available as a witness if the need should arise within a reasonable time. I was safe and free but only a few coins which Captain Braddock had given me jingled in my pocket. I would not sail again but must soon find some sort of livelihood on land.

Sad memories of the city burdened me. Nevertheless, an irresistible curiosity led me to walk the streets where I had known Jane, Frederick, and all the Olgivies I had loved in a time that now seemed far distant from me but forever near in sentiment. Thus it was that I chose to visit Mr. Stafford's workshop. But to my surprise the sign now featured the name Thomas Olgivie & Son.

Even as I stood puzzled at the change, a door opened and out walked my dear deceased friend Frederick Olgivie. He saw me before I could react, called out, and rapidly approached. I was skittish and turned to flee; persons from other spiritual realms were becoming too frequent in my life.

"Nathan, wait, it's me, Frederick!"

"But Frederick, I thought you were . . ."

"Yeah, dead, I know. Just as I thought you were. We tried to catch up to you and tell you I was alive, but you were too far ahead of us. By the time we traced you to Salem, you had already shipped out."

We hugged each other and questions poured forth about where I had been, what had happened to the Olgivies, Mr. Stafford, and the shop. He explained that Mr. Stafford had branched out into other enterprises and sold the shop to Master Olgivie. But the one question I could not bring myself to ask was about Jane. Frederick guessed my perplexity and teased me about it.

"Just on the wee chance that it may be of minor interest to

you, Nate, Jane has a fiancé who is pressuring her to marry him. He's nice enough, but she, for reasons that may have something to do with you, is unenthusiastic about the whole thing. You have returned just in time to right the ship—or maybe sink it for good—and put things in their proper order. I'm on my way home and you're coming with me. So no argument; Mother, Father, brothers and sisters, and perhaps even Jane, will want to see you."

I protested in vain—no good clothes, no haircut or shave, nothing but a long list of misadventures.

"Who cares about any of that, Nathan? The real thing is that like the Prodigal Son, you have returned to us. So come along, Mother will, so to speak, surely kill the fatted calf, and Father will put a ring on your finger and order a party in your honor, and all of us will celebrate the happy occasion. So you're coming home with me, even if I have to drag by the heels."

So with misgivings I went along. It turned out to be one of the happiest days of my life. The Olgivies all but smothered me with love and food. Master Olgivie, stalwart, kind, and firm as ever, asked me many questions about my travels and work as ship's carpenter. And with a few discreet omissions, I described them to the rapt attention of the entire family—except Jane.

Mother Olgivie, gentle and loving as ever, observed that I looked as strong as a young horse but as thin as a rail and promised as quickly as possible to remedy my excessive slenderness, which translated into her familiar terms, meant that she would ply me with food. As she began to do so that very evening.

The younger Olgivies had grown considerably but were as lovable and happy as I remembered them. I am afraid, however, that I did not pay them as much attention as they deserved. The reason for my distraction was, of course, Jane, who still had not made an appearance. Perhaps she was with her fiancé in another part of the house or on the grounds, or maybe my presence was now a matter of indifference to her. I wondered but could not ask any of these things.

After half an hour the door to her room opened and she stepped forth. I felt weak-kneed by the woman I saw. More beautiful than I remembered her, Jane came forward without hesitation, but instead of greeting me with a hug and a kiss, as her younger siblings had done, she shook my hand and asked formally about my health.

For the rest of the evening, I talked and asked questions distractedly, agitated and mystified by Jane's cool distance and aloofness. As the hour grew late and I was about to leave, Master Olgivie brought the conversation down to hard facts.

"Nathan, what are your plans now, if you can tell me?" he asked.

"Sir, all I have at the moment is a firm resolution never to go to sea again. As someone recently pointed out to me, three shipwrecks and naught to show for my voyages should be proof enough that the sailor's life is not for me. But so far that is my only firm decision. It remains to be decided where I'll go and what I'll do for a livelihood."

"There is a position open at our shop, and I imagine that with all the practical experience you have had at sea, even though you deem it profitless, will prove to be valuable knowledge. The employment is yours if you are of a mind to rejoin us."

"Master Olgivie, I am, and always will be, grateful to you

and your family for all you have done for me," I preambled, watching Jane out of the corner of my eye. "But I would not want to be a bother in any way."

"Sleep on it, Nathan, and we can discuss the matter tomorrow. Perhaps by then your way will be clearer."

As I was leaving, Jane finally called me aside and the family filed out to give us privacy. "Nathan, I know I seemed a bit standoffish with you, but as I imagine Frederick has told you, I am engaged to be married."

"Yes, so he said, but he also hinted that you do not seem to be really enthusiastic about setting a date for the wedding. Is there any chance that I may have had something to do with that?"

"When you left, I doubted I would ever see you again," she answered obliquely to my direct question.

"Does it bother you that I have come back, as Frederick says, like a returning Prodigal?"

"I am glad to see you again, Nathan."

"Only glad, nothing more?"

Her face reddened and I perceived that I had touched on a sore point and that her Scottish temper was on the rise because of my prodding questions. I was unsure of how things were going, but I felt an urgency and wanted to push as far as I could with her feelings. It might be the only chance I would have.

"Nathan, you remember enough about me to know that I don't like subtleties and indirect speech, but neither do I like being pushed."

"But indirect answers are what you're giving me."

She stared at me for a moment, then laughed and the tension between us eased a bit. "You're right, I was being evasive. I don't always practice what I preach."

"Then, Jane, let me say this: I will tell you my feelings honestly if you will then tell me yours under the same conditions."

"Fair enough, Mr. Stokes, but I must hear first what you have to say before I make any promises."

"That's fair enough for me too. I know you are engaged, and Frederick describes your fiancé as a good man. Be that as it may, I am sure you know that I love you, and I believe we were on the verge of telling each other how we felt months ago when it appeared that Frederick had died in the pinnacle disaster. My feelings for you have not changed, but instead absence has made my love grow stronger. Here's the heart of the matter: I want to marry you, to be your husband, to spend the rest of my life with you. Now, there, I have said my say; now it's time for you to say yours."

"Nathan, that's about as direct as it gets. So why deny the obvious? I promised to tell you my feelings in response to yours. You silly goose of a man, don't you know that I have been in love with from the start? All that time you were away. I prayed for you every day. My love never faltered, but finally I realized that my life had to go on and that I might never see you again. I was not even sure you were still alive. My family did not need a spinster to deal with. That's when I met Aaron. And now you show up and . . . Well, darn it, man, yes, I love you. And I don't apologize for my language. But now I have the complication with my fiancé and his feelings."

"Can't you explain to him that we knew each other before he met you? Or would you like for me to talk with him?"

"Nathan, I'm a big girl, a woman, and I can take care of my

own problems. You leave the talking part to me and do something more gainful. Get yourself to work in Daddy's shop. You'll need steady employment if you plan to be my husband and the man in my life." Then with a lovely smile she added, "And for God's sake, don't you and Frederick slip away on another boating adventure!"

I left walking on a cloud. Of course, I took Master Olgivie's offer. Of course, I asked him a few weeks later for newly unengaged Jane's hand. Of course, we were married in Boston. Of course, as everybody knows, six children were born to us in the first dozen years of our marriage. But whether we lived happily ever after, as the fairy tales go, I can't say for sure, for the "ever after part" is still happening with no end in sight.

But I have a witness that things were off to a good start. A week before Jane and I were married in June, eight months after my return, I asked her to go for a walk with me on the Boston Common. The day was warm and Bostonians were out in force. I noticed a familiar man of substantial girth and a shock of red hair dressed elegantly in the old style doling out handfuls of nuts and seeds from a bag to a troop of scurrying squirrels and fluttering birds. As before, his gold ring with the magnificent turquoise caught my eye. He smiled and waved his hand which I took as a gesture that all was well and on the right track. I stopped, bowed in his direction, and thanked him in my best manner.

"Darling, did you speak to someone just now?" Jane asked.

"Yes, so I did, my darling, to the gentleman sitting on the bench back there feeding the birds and squirrels. I've had some dealings with him."

Jane looked back and frowned. "Nathan, all I see are birds

and squirrels. There's no one there."

I looked too and was not surprised to see that he was gone. "My friend is a very busy person," I explained to her. "He has a way of rushing off suddenly like that to take care of things."

CHAPTER 6

After vowing never to sail again, I was puzzled to find myself again on the high seas and couldn't remember how I got there. At first the waters around the vessel were calm and warm, but then suddenly the skies darkened and the winds whipped up and began tossing the ship and thrumming the sails. I reached for the nearest handrail to steady myself and tried to remember the name of the vessel, its tonnage, captain, and cargo. All I knew was that it had the feel of a solid craft, but my mind was a blank on everything else. Maybe I had been shanghaied, but that possibility was as murky as the rest of my new experience. I heard excited voices and wondered if we were in for a storm.

Then one voice rose above the rest, and my surprise grew when I seemed to recognize its familiar sound. It was the feminine voice of someone I knew and she was calling my name as the waves got rougher and tossed me back and forth.

"Nathan, Nathan, wake up! Nathan!"

I awoke with a start. The seas and ship faded and the shaking stopped. I looked up into my girlfriend Jane's beautiful blue eyes.

"Where am I?" I asked, still dazed.

"At Epcot, dummy," she laughed, "at the American Pavilion fountain, dead to the world on a bench in front of that kiosk over there, but from what you were saying in your dreams you were still adventuring somewhere out on the deep blue sea."

"Man, I was sound asleep all right, and you're right, I was

dreaming I was on an old sailing ship and it was tossing and yawing in the waves."

"That was me trying to shake you awake."

"Jane, it was the weirdest dream, almost too real to be a dream. It was like a sequel to my adventure yesterday."

"Well, my love, I'm not surprised. All you talked about last evening was your Epcot adventure. This dream sounds like more of the same. You talked so much about your adventure yesterday that your family was about ready to leave you at the hotel today. Even your sweet, mild mannered mother and sister Pamela were ready to scream last evening. Promise me you won't retell it today. Promise?"

"Sorry about that, darling. Maybe that delicious Boston clam chowder they served me at the Kiosk had something to do with it. I never expected to find chowder in Florida half as good as our real Boston chowder. But it was nice to be surprised. But, hey, I do promise to lay off my adventure story and talk about something else today. You have to understand, though, that the adventure was a lot like the stories my four times great grandfather wrote about in his memoirs. I've read them several times and identify a lot with him. His name was Nathan Stokes, just like mine, and he married a woman named Jane, too, just as I'm going to do when we get back to Boston. You're too pretty to be walking around alone with all the guys hanging out to grab you if I'm not around."

"Is that intention a threat or a promise?"

"I guess that depends on you, Jane. All I know is that I want you to be my wife. You have my ring and my honorable intentions, as they used to say in the old days. So with that said, what say we go and find the others and grab some lunch?"

"Sounds like a plan I can live with on all counts, hubby-to-be. But before we go, there're two other things I need to do to you."

"Is that a threat or a promise?"

"You'll decide when I do them. First, this."

She kissed him.

"And now the other. Nate, you have given me several nice things, best of all my engagement ring, and I haven't really given you much of anything. So here, I want you to have this."

She handed him a small, ribbon-laced package.

"What is it?"

"Open it and see."

It was a gorgeous turquoise ring, exactly like the one the mysterious redheaded stranger had in his adventure.

"You've told me that your ancestors appreciated turquoise above all other stones. So I thought it might be appropriate."

"You don't know how much, Jane. You couldn't have picked anything better. So thanks and more thanks," he said, giving her a kiss. "The old Cherokees and other Native Americans believed turquoise was a good luck stone, able to ward off evil and bring good luck. But it's almost spooky that you would give me a ring exactly like the one I saw on my benefactor's hand in my adventure. Despite all the talking I did, I don't think I mentioned it."

"It is a little scary. I guess it means that we're beginning to read each other's thoughts. Does that bother you?"

"Not a bit, Madam mind reader, but you still have a long way to go."

"Why do you say that?"

"If you were really into my head, you would know how

hungry I am. So come on, let's go find the others and have a good lunch. After that we can start getting ready for our next adventure."

A Mouse Gate Adventure Book
What's your adventure?

www.mousegate.com

Title: Louisiana Rogue
- Author: Harold Raley
- Publisher: Lamar University Press
- Paper Back: ISBN: 9780985255275
- eBook: Kindle
- Pages 306
- Publication Date: April 2013

This wonderfully entertaining picaresque novel by Harold Raley falls in the tradition of rogue literature established by Tom Jones and other early novels. Set in the nineteenth century, Louisiana Rogue will take you on a wild, fast-paced romp through all levels of Cajun society in the 1830s. The title page says the book promises to tell "The Life and Times of Pierre Prospère-Tourmoulin, Picket-pocket, Thief, Gambler, Fugitive, Undertaker, Barber, Doctor, Priest, Prisoner, Bandit, and Count; Latterly penned in his hand for the gentle reader of leisure, Spanning the years 1831-1839" and claims to be translated by Peter Tourmoulin.

Title: The Unknown God: Mysteries of Deity, Time, Space, and Creation

- Author: Harold Raley
- Publisher: CreateSpace
- Paper Back: ISBN: 9781466273184
- Pages 142
- Publication Date: October, 2011

In his powerful Introduction to The Unknown God, religious thinker and writer Harold Raley makes this unusual request of the reader: "Suspend, if you will, everything you know about God. Put aside for the duration of this reading your traditional theologies and hear a new and more reverent way of thinking about God. When you return to your old understandings, they will have deeper meanings, unless those you once professed were meaningless to start with. If you are unwilling or unable to do as I ask, read no further. This message is not for you. The truth it contains will find you later when it is ready for you and you have been made ready for it." To approach Deity from this radically new perspective--arguably the greatest advance in theological thought of modern times--is to expose and shed light on the baffling paradoxes, improbable notions, and misleading errors not only about God but also about time, space, creation, and immortality. In each of these categories this book offers stunning new insights that incorporate not only the efforts of classical theologians but also the latest discoveries in science. Outline in these advanced insights is a new understanding of human life. By the law of corresponding identities, Raley explains, a more elevated theory of God necessarily means a more elevated theory of mankind. Each of the many themes and aperçus packed into this slender volume could have been a hefty tome. With pristine eloquence Raley reduces them to the essentials, believing as he does that clarity of style is courtesy to the reader.

Title: The Light of Eden:
A Christian Worldview
- Author: Harold Raley
- Publisher: John M. Hardy Publishing Co
- Paper Back: ISBN: 9780979839122
- Pages 196
- Publication Date: May 2008

An inspiring vision of richer Christian life and thought. In the tradition of C. S. Lewis and G. K. Chesterton, this extraordinary book is both a spiritual adventure and an intellectual feast. Packed with illuminating insights and written in beautiful language, The Light of Eden introduces its readers to a vast treasury of creative ideas, innovative concepts, and possibilities contained in Christianity.

Title: The Spirit of Spain

• Author: Harold Raley
• Publisher: Halcyon Pr Ltd
• Paper Back: ISBN: 9780970605498
• Pages 212
• Publication Date: October, 2011

The Spirit of Spain brims with aperçus and revelations, many of them controversial, others startling, all engrossing. From Roman Hispania to the most recent Spanish trends, Professor Raley narrates the unique story of Spanish civilization. Examples of his original thinking include a "phenomenology of Spanish history," a new theory of the Spanish Renaissance, new concepts of Spanish patriotism and nationalism, and a reinterpretation of Spanish "Stoicism." As the book unfolds he also takes many sidelong looks into Hispanic America and offers a new explanation of Spain's relationship to Moslem Al-Andalus and modern Europe. The book culminates in a radical analysis of "Quixotic life" and its unsuspected significance for the post-modern age.

Title: Barefoot On A Frosty Morn
- Author: Harold Raley
- Publisher: Mouse Gate Press
- Paper Back: ISBN: 9781590953426
- eBook ISBN: 9781590953433
- Pages 352
- Publication Date: October, 2016

Barefoot on a Frosty Morn is a literary and genealogical tapestry of several families over three centuries. The genealogical threads stretch back to England and France and unfold in step with America's continental expansion. The families crisscross north, south, and west as the tapestry grows in richness and complexity. A final episode sheds light on the earliest roots of the story. The reader has a perspective only partially available to the personalities immersed in the stories. Episodes are woven around some American milestones: the Revolution, the Civil War and WWII. These resonate and enrich but do not hinder the genealogical flow of the novel. In its conception and execution *Barefoot on a Frosty Morn* is unlike any writing before it. It surpasses the limits of history and narrates the essence of the American vision of life.

Title: The Prodigal
- Author: Harold Raley
- Publisher: Mouse Gate Press
- Paper Back: ISBN: 9781590953402
- eBook ISBN: 9781590953419
- Pages 96
- Publication Date: October, 2016

In the tradition of Crusoe and Sabatini, The Prodigal is a story of the shipwreck and struggle for survival of a young ship's carpenter who escapes one captivity only to fall into more dangerous circumstances. The story unfolds from Boston to Mexico, Cuba, Africa, and back again. At critical points a mysterious stranger intervenes to lend a hand and guide him to his destiny.

www.ingramcontent.com/pod-product-compliance
Lightning Source LLC
Chambersburg PA
CBHW020533120726
47904CB00003B/1063